AMIAYA ENTERTAINMENT LLC

Presents

A Diamond
In the Rough

A Novel
by

James "I-God Allah" Morris

Copyright ©2005 by James Morris
Written by James Morris for
Amiaya Entertainment LLC
Published by Amiaya Entertainment LLC
Edited by Antoine "Inch" Thomas
Cover Design by Marion Designs
Printed in The United States America

ISBN: 0-9745075-4-7
[1. Urban-Fiction   2. Drama-Fiction   3. Brooklyn-Fiction]

Dedication

**This book is dedicated to my wife
Queen Star-Asia for her years of support
mentally, physically, morally and spiritually.**

U-N-I VERSE

It won't be long now.
Also to my beautiful seeds.
Quatasia Shahqueen, Divine I-Asiatic,
Bishmi Allah, He-Allah Supreme,
My-Queen Medina, Lil Eternal I-God
and I-Paradise Jewel.
Without y'all who am I?
Y'all are my strength and hope.

Acknowledgements

I have learned throughout my walk through trials and tribulations that many may come but only a few are chosen. I would like to thank and give a strong bulletproof love to my wife who stood by me throughout these stressful years of my incarceration. It's been a long journey, Queen, Born-universal-truth (but) we made it. U-N-I VERSE! To all of my seeds: QUATASIA SHAHQUEEN, DIVINE ASIATIC, BISHMI ALLAH, HE-ALLAH SUPREME, MY-QUEEN MEDINA, LIL ETERNAL I-GOD, and I-PARADISE JEWEL. WHO AM I WITHOUT Y'ALL? Daddy's home now! To my physical brother, I-See Allah. Keep your head up, Lord, I got you. Believe me, I know the days are long in those hells, born-u-truth they can't stop night and day, and as long as that's being manifest, your time will come. To my mother-in-law, nothing but love and respect forever. I will never forget the love you showed my family during my absence. I love you as if you were my mother. Ms. Sheena, thank you for all you have done for me and mine. One love to all of my numerous cousins, nieces, nephews, aunts and uncles. Aunt Poppie, I love you. Janice, you know how we do, one love to you and Jayquan. To all my brothers and sisters, nothing but love. Keba Cheba!

All praises are due to the father Allah and Justice. To the nation of Gods and Earths. Siheem, I love you Godbody. Sincere, Bornmaster, Sha-sha, Tamu, Bornsupreme, I-Self Allah, Eternal, Divine Magnetic, Jahid, Born Everlasting, Tislam, I

Am, Hamel, and all the brothers and sisters who have walked the miles with me. Proper Education, Always, Correct, Errors. To the God Love Eternal. God, your word was Bond and I thank you for holding me down for all of these years. One love!

Special acknowledgement to my Amiaya Family. Inch and Tania, thank you for making this thing possible for me and my family and making us a part of your family. Forever I will hold y'all down.

A Bulletproof love to all the brothers and sisters that are still on lock down in state and federal prison who held their heads and are doing their time respectfully without falling victim to the devil's civilization.

Peace and blessing to the mothers of my children outside of my wife for playing the part of their father and mother to them while I was incarcerated. I'm Home Now! It's my time to play my part.

To all my readers, I thank you. Peace!

"It is only when a rough **Diamond** is faceted that its brilliance and beauty are revealed to the naked eye."

Prologue

"Bitch, why the fuck are you always stressing a nigga? Don't worry about where I've been or who I've been with. All you need to worry about is me paying all the fucking bills and coming home to your sorry ass and this spoiled bastard little bitch." Rahmel was pacing the room.

"Rahmel, I'm sorry that you feel your daughter is a bastard little bitch. Why don't you just leave us be?" Angel, Diamond's mother, was standing in the middle of the living room with little Diamond behind her. She was pleading with Diamond's father.

"Bitch!" he screamed. His eyes were wide and his temper flared.

Smack!!! Rahmel cocked his hand back to take another swing.

"Mommy! Mommy! Daddy, please, nooooo! Please Daddy, don't hit Mommy no more." Diamond was now standing between her mother and father with her tiny arms draped around both of their legs.

"Little bitch, you wanna take up for your sorry ass mother, huh?" Rahmel looked down at Diamond.

Smack!!! Diamond caught one upside her head.

She cried, "Daddy, noooo!"

"Bitch, shut up." Pop Dukes went nuts after that.

Smack!!!

Diamond jumped up in a cold sweat. She sat up in her

bed and gazed around her room. Diamond had another one of the same dreams she'd been having for years. She got out of her bed and walked into her mother's room to check on her mom. Angel was sound asleep with the TV on. Diamond turned the TV off and gave her mother a kiss on the forehead. "I love you," Diamond said in a whisper.

Diamond was haunted by the same images of her mother being abused by her father for years. Growing up and living with her father, Diamond watched the abuse of her mother grow until it became unbearable. But once Rahmel started abusing Diamond, Angel knew they had to get away from him before he killed one of them. Times were hard for Diamond and her mother but they had each other and that was the greatest riches they could have. The best part was that they didn't have to worry about Rahmel's abuse anymore. It had been over three years and Rahmel didn't know where they lived. And with that, they were comfortable. They made by with what they had. Diamond looked at the clock on the wall and noticed that it was past midnight.

"Damn, it's after 12. It's my birthday," Diamond said to herself as she walked back into the room and jumped back into her bed. *I wonder what Brooklyn is doing right now. She's probably giving some perverted old dude a lap dance.* Diamond thought to herself as she laid back and put her head back under the covers so she could try to get back to sleep. She had to meet Big Ben in the morning...

Chapter 1
A Gift of Diamonds

"Yeah! Huhh, yeah, yeah! Diamond, right there, that's how I like it, bitch. Right there. This pussy is tight. Come on, turn over. Let me get into this young pussy," Big Ben ejected his manhood from Diamond's sugar walls and turned her over on her back.

Diamond laid on her back with her legs spread thinking about the new DKNY sneakers she was going to buy with the money she got from Big Ben, while he laid on top of her handling his business. Diamond wished he'd hurry up and cum because she wasn't enjoying herself at all and never did. Whenever she had sex with Big Ben she always thought about other things. Big Ben was about 360 pounds of fat. His stomach looked as if he was in his last semester of pregnancy. But his money was long. Whenever Diamond spent time with Big Ben she knew she was guaranteed at least three hundred dollars.

Diamond had just turned eighteen, but had the body of a twenty-seven year old woman. Diamond was golden brown with long jet-black hair, and a small mole on the top of her lip which complemented her dimples. Diamond lived with her mother Angel, who was a mix between black and Hispanic. Angel was fifteen years her senior. Her father, Rahmel, was major in the drug trade. Her parents had separated because Rahmel was a womanizer and an abuser. He had three other families. All of Diamond's siblings were younger than she was, but she was Angel's *only* child.

Life for them was hard in Brooklyn. The streets were her only escape. Diamond had witnessed her mother being abused by Rahmel for years. She always wondered why her mother never just left. She could remember a time when her mother first found out that Rahmel had other children. When she approached him on the issue, a big fight broke out. Rahmel had beaten Angel like she was a dude. This soon became a regular activity in the house. The straw that broke the camel's back was when Angel came home and found Rahmel in the bed with her next door neighbor. Once Rahmel left the house, Angel packed her and Diamond's things, left and they never looked back. They moved into a shelter for battered women until they were able to find themselves an apartment in a building for families in crises. Times were rough for them and they never received any financial support from Rahmel.

Angel worked as a cashier at a local Key Foods supermarket where she made just enough for the very bare necessities: rent, food, bills and clothes to put on their backs. Diamond knew that her mother was struggling so she tried not to bother her with too much. She had Big Ben and all he wanted was some pussy and after four or five minutes, he was cumming. She earned enough money for school clothes and she could help her mother out as well. Every Friday and Saturday, Diamond could count on Big Ben's date. So from Big Ben alone, she made a pretty good amount of money.

"Ohh, Ben, yes, Ben! Right there, Daddy! Fuck this pussy!"

Diamond said every now and then to stroke Ben's ego.

Ben didn't do anything at all to stimulate any pleasure in Diamond. He just got on top of her and did him. Every now and then he would eat the pussy. That would be okay, but the fat mutha fucka didn't know what he was doing. The only time Diamond ever had an orgasm was when she and her best friend, Brooklyn, had a little girl-to-girl rendezvous. They weren't bisexuals; they were just curious. Diamond was strictly dickly while Brooklyn did it all. And Brooklyn definitely knew how to make Diamond feel like a real woman. Outside of that and her masturbating, today was her birthday and Big Ben said he had something special for her. *I hope he wasn't talking about this sloppy ass head he's attempting to give me*, Diamond thought to herself as Big Ben went down on her.

"Ohh, Ben, yes, right there!" once again Diamond said to stroke Ben's ego.

"You like that, ma?" Ben mumbled with a mouth full of Diamond's coochie.

"Yes, Daddy, come on, give me some more of that dick." Diamond was getting upset that Ben was teasing her pussy with his non-pussy eating ass. She wanted him to hurry up and cum so she could be out.

Ben told Diamond to turn back over on all fours where he started hitting it and smacking her ass rushing him to cum. Ben rolled over on the bed. Diamond was relieved that it was over.

"Did you like that, Diamond?" Ben asked as he lit his Newport.

"Yes, Big Ben, I see why they call you Big Ben!" Diamond said, lying once again. She bashfully rolled her eyes at him.

"What 'cha doing today?" he asked, exhaling smoke from his nostrils.

"I'm just gonna do a little shopping with my home girl," Diamond said as she got up and went into the bathroom to wash up.

Diamond felt nasty after she had sex with Big Ben. Big Ben had a certain odor about himself that he carried because he was so big. It turned Diamond's stomach, but after a while, she got used to it. As Diamond came out of the bathroom, she looked at Big Ben's fat ass lying across the bed looking like a beached whale and thought to herself that she had to find a better way to make a living because after today, she was through with Big Ben.

"Hey, Ben, I'm about to leave now."

"Aye, Diamond, didn't I tell you that I had a surprise for your birthday?" Big Ben said as he reached in his dresser drawer and pulled out a box from Jacob the jeweler.

I know this fat nigga didn't buy me something from Jacob. I might have to fuck with this nasty nigga a little longer, Diamond thought to herself as Ben passed her the box.

When she opened the box, it was a Jacob watch, flooded with diamonds.

"You can't have a name like Diamond without any diamonds," Big Ben said.

Diamond jumped on top of Big Ben and gave him a kiss and sucked on his neck. She knew after this that he was gonna expect some pussy, or even worse, he probably wanted her to suck on his nasty sour smelling dick. Diamond had never sucked a dick before, but she knew she could from watching pornos. Porno tapes were how she became educated about sex. One time she came into her mother's room and caught her performing oral sex on her father. Rahmel looked like he was trying to choke her mother to death. When she burst into the room and Angel tried to stop, Rahmel just held onto her mother's long hair and wouldn't let her go until he came all over her face. Diamond hated her father and if Big Ben wanted that done, she wouldn't do it.

Diamond had met Big Ben a couple of months before while she was with her best friend, Brooklyn, in the Alby Square Mall, in downtown Brooklyn on Fulton Street. They were downtown window shopping and talking to guys. Big Ben was coming out of the jewelry store where Diamond and Brooklyn were admiring some earrings in the window. Big Ben walked up to Diamond and asked her did she see anything she liked? Diamond told him that she liked the bamboo earrings. Big Ben introduced himself and asked Diamond that if he bought her the earrings, would she go out with him. Diamond was only seventeen at the time, but she was built like she was much older. Diamond told Big Ben she was twenty. Ben bought Diamond the earrings and they had been meeting up every week ever since. To Diamond, Big Ben was her meal ticket. But now he had spent a couple of thousand on this watch, which meant that Ben was expecting more.

"Diamond, you know you're my lil shorty now. I don't want you running around with your little chicken head friend Brooklyn chasing guys around. I got something else for you," Big Ben said as he handed Diamond a pager and a cell phone. "This is so that whenever I come back in town I can reach you with no problem." Ben was showing Diamond the beeper as if it were a rare artifact.

Big Ben hustled in upstate Poughkeepsie, New York. He had a couple of crack spots up there. He was originally from Brooklyn but he moved up state. He still had his mother who lived in the Weeksville Houses on Troy Avenue, but Ben's money was kinda long, so he splurged.

Diamond couldn't wait to leave Big Ben's fat ass. As soon as she got outside, she called Brooklyn. Brooklyn was one of Diamond's best and only friends. Brooklyn was a nineteen-year-old Puerto Rican mommy who grew up in an all-black neighborhood, Bedstuy. She didn't speak any Spanish. Her real name was Maria, but she told everybody her name was Brooklyn. Brooklyn stripped at a local strip club in Queens. Brooklyn had a one-year-old son that her grandmother took care of. Brooklyn was Diamond's road dog. She lived in her grandmother's brownstone. Her mother had recently died of AIDS. She had been a heroin addict. Brooklyn was named after her grandmother, Ms. Maria. She had taken care of all her grandchildren. Brooklyn also had two older brothers that were in prison.

"Yo, girl, what's up?" Diamond questioned on the other end of the phone.

"Who's this?" Brooklyn asked sounding like she just got up.

"Girl, it's me. Get your butt up."

"Diamond, what time is it?" Brooklyn stretched and tried to focus in on her clock.

"It's after 2 p.m.! I'm coming over. I got something to show you girl. Get up, it's my birthday," Diamond said sounding all excited.

"Girl, it feels like I just went to bed. I got in around six this morning. I'm tired."

"Girl, just open the door. I'm on my way," Diamond said before she hung up her cell phone.

Diamond had to stop off at her house and check on her mother first. Their telephone was cut off so Diamond was gonna give Angel the fifty dollars to pay the bill. Her mother was a good person—it's just that Rahmel *destroyed* her. He had abused her for fifteen years until she got enough strength to leave him. Rahmel was the main provider. Angel was fifteen when she left home to be with Rahmel. She got pregnant and dropped out of school to be a full-time mother and a housewife to Rahmel. So when she had Rahmel locked up, which is when she made her escape, she was forced to fend for her and Diamond all by herself for the first time. Angel was thirty-three years old and still had a youthful look about herself, but the marks from her abusive relationship still showed through her scars and the permanent black eye she had. Diamond loved her mother more than life and always wondered why she put up with Rahmel's abuse.

They stayed in a grey apartment building on Bergen and Franklin in Crown Heights. The building was for women and children who were abused by their husbands or spouses. They lived on the second floor in a two-bedroom apartment.

When Diamond walked into the apartment, Angel was sitting on the couch watching her soaps on TV.

"Diamond, where have you been?" Angel asked as she noticed the sparkle from Diamond's wrist.

"I've been out." Diamond smiled when she noticed her mom staring at her watch.

"Who gave you that?" Angel said pulling Diamond's wrist to her face for a closer look.

"Big Ben gave it to me."

Diamond told her mother of Big Ben, but she never told her that Ben was a year younger than she was.

"Girl, where that boy get that kind of money from?"

"Ma, I don't ask. The *least* I know, the better I am," Diamond said as she counted out seventy-five dollars and gave it to her mother. "Ma, fifty is for the phone bill and twenty-five is for some groceries."

Angel took the money and put it in her bra and turned her attention back to her soaps while Diamond left to go find her friend Brooklyn.

As she walked across town to Brooklyn's house, Pop, a dude that hustled on the corner, pulled Diamond's arm.

"What's up, Diamond?" he asked. "When you gonna let a nigga get with you? I'll take care of you!" Pop said as he pulled out a mitt of money.

"Nigga, you don't have enough to take care of me. Besides, I don't think you can handle this," Diamond said and kept walking.

"Yeah, but you giving that pussy up to that fat nigga driving that Lex, huh? You keep bringing that nigga around here and I'ma get 'em," Pop said as he gave his man a pound.

When Diamond reached Brooklyn's house, Brooklyn was still in the bed. Brooklyn's grandmother, Brooklyn's son and a few more little cousins all lived downstairs. Brooklyn shared the apartment with her aunt.

Diamond ran and jumped on Brooklyn's bed. Brooklyn snatched the covers off her head with a dazed look on her face.

"Bitch, what's wrong with you?" Brooklyn asked as she tried to regain her composure. "You scared the shit out of me." She was squinting from the light.

"Bitch, I told you I was coming by. Besides, look what that fat mutha fucka bought me for my birthday," Diamond said as she showed Brooklyn her Jacob watch.

"Ah, shit, bitch, did you suck that fat nigga's dick or something? You nasty hoe!" Brooklyn said. She screamed, bugging out at how many diamonds the watch had.

"Nah, that nigga want me to be his girl. I got 'em whipped with this diamond between my legs," Diamond said as she got off the bed and went into her purse to show Brooklyn what else

Big Ben gave her. "Look, the nigga even gave me a pager and a cell phone, so he could reach me."

"Diamond, I don't know how you fuck with that fat nigga," Brooklyn said admiring the beeper and telephone.

"Because, he got money and he's not afraid to trick it on me. These broke ass niggas around here don't have nothing to offer. That broke nigga Pop on the corner of my block tried to holla at me today. He even had the nerve to pull out his little knot of money. I wanted to flash my watch on the nigga and be like, *nigga if you can't flood me with diamonds, you can't even smell the coochie,*" Diamond said as she and Brooklyn laughed.

"Yo, girl, what ever happened to that producer that do music for the Roc that gave you his number at that party last week? Did you ever call him?" Brooklyn asked as she took a second look at Diamond's watch.

"Yeah, girl, me and him have been talking, but we haven't hooked up yet. He's in Atlanta right now, but he'll be back next week."

"Girl, that nigga is kinda fine. You better get with him before I do," Brooklyn said as she went into the bathroom to wash up.

"Bitch, hurry up, I wanna go get them new DKNY sneakers at the mall."

"Bitch, you know I have to get my wake-me-up before I do anything," Brooklyn said as she got a blunt and a bag of weed out of her purse and gave it to Diamond to roll. She went into the bathroom to wash up and brush her teeth.

When Brooklyn came out of the bathroom, Diamond had finished rolling the weed and was lighting the blunt.

"Girl, I met this fine nigga at the club last night. He spent 'bout 250 on lap dances with me alone. He gave me his number and you know I don't really deal with niggas that come to the club, but this nigga was fine," Brooklyn said as she walked out of the bathroom and turned on her R. Kelly CD.

"Girl, did you see this nigga on that tape? That nigga is a freak, huh?" Brooklyn asked. She wondered to herself what it would be like had it been her on that tape and not that other girl.

"Bitch, please, you just wish that was you!" Diamond spoke and caught Brooklyn's smile.

"True that, but as soon as that nigga tried that pissing on me shit, his ass would have been out."

Diamond and Brooklyn smoked the blunt while Brooklyn got dressed. Diamond's pager went off while Brooklyn was pulling on her pants.

Beep. Beep. Beep. Beep!!!

"What, bitch, that nigga paging you already?" Brooklyn was wiggling her waist trying to fit her thick ass into a pair of jeans that were two sizes too small.

"Yeah, child, please, and they say Diamonds are a *girls* best friend, please! I got that fat nigga whipped," Diamond said as she pulled out her cell phone to call Big Ben back.

"What's up, Ben?" Diamond said in her most sexual voice.

"Yo, what time are you gonna be finished shopping?"

"Around 6 p.m., why?" Diamond passed the blunt to Brooklyn.

"Because, I need you to make a move with me somewhere, aight? Make sure you page me as soon as you finish. Aight? One!" Big Ben hung up his phone before Diamond could answer.

As Diamond hung up, she wondered what it could be that Big Ben wanted her to do. *Damn, I hope this nigga don't want me to fuck him any more today.* Diamond thought to herself as she reached for the blunt from Brooklyn.

"Girl, I wish you would hurry up," Diamond said as she looked at her watch and admired the shine. "Bitch, I got to be back around 6 p.m. That nigga want me to do something for him. I knew when he gave me this watch he was gonna be a pain in my ass."

"Diamond, please, that fat nigga got that thing on lock. Come on, I'm ready," Brooklyn said as she snatched her keys off the dresser.

As they walked to the train station on Utica, an all-black H2 Hummer pulled up banging the Lox's song, *Money, Power, Respect.*

"Yo, Brooklyn!" the duo stopped.

"Damn, girl, who's that?" Diamond jerked her head, clearing the hair from her face. She wanted whoever was driving the luxury SUV to notice that Brooklyn wasn't alone.

"Oh, hey, Divine," Brooklyn said as she ran up to the truck.

"Yo, where y'all going?" he looked out the window over Brooklyn's head. Divine took a peek at Diamond, then brought his attention back to Brooklyn.

"Me and my girl is going downtown to do some shopping," Brooklyn blushed, hoping that Divine noticed her hint that she wanted a ride.

"Y'all want a ride?" Divine threw his truck into *park.*

"Hell, yeah, hold on, let me tell my girl," Brooklyn said as she walked back to where she left Diamond standing. "Girl, that's the nigga I was telling you about from the club last night. He's gonna drive us downtown, come on." She waved Diamond on.

As they got into the car, Brooklyn introduced Divine to Diamond.

"Yo, go in the ashtray and light that blunt up, ya heard? That's that shit from Cooper and Broadway," Divine said as he pulled off.

"What's up, Divine? Where are you on your way to?" Brooklyn asked as she lit the blunt.

"I'm just trying to kill some time before I meet up with my man to handle some business." Divine paused, looked at the traffic in his rearview mirror, switched lanes, then diverted his questions back to Brooklyn. "So what's up, Brooklyn? When are we gonna hook up on some personal time outside of the club?"

"You tell me, Divine. After I come from downtown I'm free until I have to go to the club tonight." She stole another glance at the baller.

"How much would you charge me to take the night off?" This brought an even bigger smile to Brooklyn's face. When Divine asked the question, he peeked at Diamond through the rearview mirror and caught her smiling at her best friend.

"I don't know. How much do you think I'm worth?" Brooklyn asked as she passed the blunt to Diamond.

"Brooklyn, it's not that much money in the world to pay a woman for what she's truly worth."

"Oh, that is so sweet," Diamond said as she passed the blunt back up front.

"Divine, I'ma page you around 10 for you to come get me, aight?"

"Okay, Brooklyn, page me and I promise you, you won't regret it," Divine said as he pulled in front of Juniors and let them out. "Diamond, nice meeting you. Brooklyn, I'll see you later," Divine said as he pulled off.

Chapter 2
Move Making

Big Ben pulled up on Diamond's block. He told Diamond to be downstairs in front of her building at exactly 8:15. Ben didn't like the vibe he got from the cats on Diamond's block that stood in front of the corner store. It was the same cats looking at him crazy whenever he came to pick Diamond up. Ben wasn't no gangsta. Whenever shit got out of hand for him he would pay some of the young guns from around his way to handle his beef. Ben wanted to make the money without the drama that came with it. That was one of the main reasons he went upstate to hustle. The streets of Brooklyn were a little too grimy for him. As of last week, Ben had made preparations to open up shop down in N.C. Today he was to meet up with his connect and purchase some weight. Ben was used to copping a key here and there, but today his connect told him that he had some good deals for him if he was serious about what he was doing. His connect told Ben that he would give him a key for 9.5, but he would have to buy at least 10 at a time. Ben had to jump on that because currently he was paying 19.5 and getting 24.5 for one. In N.C. he could get 31. He could triple his money. When his little cousin told him how fruitful the money was in N.C. he knew he had to make that move. Ben would put Diamond on the Amtrak or the Greyhound that evening and he would drive down there to meet her. He'd give her at least 5 g's for each trip and he'd get to tear the pussy up for her as soon as they get down there.

Big Ben was distracted from his thoughts by a knock on the window.

"Oh, what's up, Diamond? Get in," Ben said as he unlocked the doors.

"Damn, Ben! Why's all the windows closed and the doors locked?" Diamond asked as she got in.

"Diamond, I told you to be downstairs in fifteen minutes, that I was on my way. Why them niggas at the corner of your block always looking at me funny when I come to pick you up?"

"They're nobody but the dudes that live on the block and they hustle on the corner. Plus, I had to do something for my mother, you know, it's only me and her. When you called and asked me to go out of town with you, you know she wasn't trying to hear that."

"Did you tell her that we're just going out there to do some shopping? And that you'll be back tomorrow."

"Yeah, but my moms is not stupid. She knows the deal. You know that she's only a couple of years older than you are," Diamond said as she pushed the cigarette lighter in so she could light the half blunt Ben had in the ashtray. "Ben, where are we going where I don't have to bring any change of clothes?"

"We'll be right back tomorrow, but I'm not going with you."

"What?!" Diamond sat up in her seat.

"I'm going with you, but I'm not gonna ride the bus with

you. I'ma meet you down there," Ben said as he pulled off. He turned at the light and noticed one of the cats on the corner say something to his man and then point at his car.

Fifteen minutes later, Ben pulled up in front of an apartment building on Hancock and Ralph not too far from the Brooklyn house. The block was full of activity. You could tell that a lot of drugs were sold there. Ben told Diamond to hang out in the car until he got back; he'd be but a couple of minutes. Ben got out of the car and walked into the building. As soon as he entered the building, two dudes with guns checked him for weapons, then told him to go upstairs to the second floor, apartment 2A. When Ben entered the apartment, his connect was sitting at a table smoking a blunt, counting money.

"Yo, Big Ben! What's up, son? What's going on?" He looked at his potential gold mine.

"What's up, Vine? It's your world, baby, I'm just a squirrel trying to get a nut! Ya heard?" Ben said as he gave Divine a pound.

"Nah, son, it's not my world. I'm just trying to survive and duck the feds, yo. Here, have a seat, big man. What you drinking?" Divine asked as he told his man to bring the suitcases.

"Yo, Vine, I'm alright. I just wanna handle this so I can make some moves because I have somebody waitin' in the car downstairs for me," Ben said as he pulled out four stacks of money from his Jan sports bag.

As Divine counted the money, he told Ben about the little Spanish shorty he had met at the club the night before.

"Yo shorty is right, all she needs is a nigga like me to get her right. Ya heard? A nigga like me will clean her up and have niggas mouths dropping when she walk by."

"Yeah, Vine, I got me a little hood rat myself, but you

know I got to keep her on a leash. Because them young girls fall in love too quick and easy. I can't have that get back to wifey," Ben said as Divine's man entered back into the room with two suitcases.

Divine passed his man the pile of money and proceeded to lay ten keys on the table in front of Ben. Divine then pulled out a key chain with a small spoon attached to it and passed it to Ben so he could sample the product.

Ben took a sample and rubbed it on his gums and teeth. He then sniffed a spoonful. The whole left side of his face went numb.

"Yo, dog! That's that raw shit there, son!" Ben said as he sat back in the chair to catch his composure.

"Son, I told you I got that shit for you. Ben, let me ask you something on the serious note. Do you have a place where you can really get rid of the work? Because if you do, I can take care of you whereas we could both get rich."

Ben leaned up. "Yeah, Vine, I wouldn't fuck with it if I didn't."

"Aight, check this out," Divine said as he waved for his man to come over to them. "I'ma give you five more of them things on consignment and there's plenty more where that came from. As long as you can get rid of it, I'll keep it coming."

Divine told his man to bring five more as Ben rolled a blunt of the Hydro that Divine had on the table. Ben kept looking at his watch because he knew that Diamond had to be on the bus by 11:45.

"Yo, son, why you keep looking at your watch? You ain't lose none of the ice in the mutha fucka," Divine said as he passed Ben a light for the blunt.

"Nah, it's not that fam, I got my little runner in the car and she got to catch the Greyhound."

"Aight, son, I'm not gonna keep you much longer," Divine said as his man walked back into the room with five more of them things.

Ben packed everything nice and neatly in one suitcase and told Divine that he'd hit him back in a couple of days. Ben was nervous leaving Divine's building with all of them keys of crack. He was more afraid of the dudes in front of the building than he was of getting caught or pulled over by the police. When he reached the car, he was relieved. He put the suitcase in the back of the whip and pulled off.

Ben drove straight to the bus station.

"Diamond, if you pull into the station and I'm not there waiting for you, call this number. I should reach down there before you but just in case, this is my aunt's number. They'll be expecting you."

"Hold up, Ben. You better make sure your ass is down there when I get off that bus. You bet not have me stranded down south with all of these drugs assed out," Diamond said.

"Don't worry. I said *just* in case I don't beat you down there. But I'll be there, don't worry. Here, this is for your ticket and this is yours."

Ben gave Diamond a total of 5 g's. Diamond, having that money in her hands, built her courage and was ready to go.

She jumped on the bus headed for N.C. She had five keys of work and five thousand dollars. She could say fuck the fat mutha fucka and she and Brooklyn could flip it themselves and be set, but as quick as she had the thought, just as quick, it was dismissed. Because neither she nor Brooklyn knew the first thing about selling drugs. *Where would they sell it? To whom? For how much?* They knew nothing. So fuck it. She'll just get the fat mutha fucka for all he had.

• • •

Brooklyn took the night off from dancing at the club on the request of Divine. Tonight she could have made a killing at the club, anywhere from five hundred to seven hundred dollars because it was the weekend and the club would be packed. Thursdays, Fridays and Saturdays were her money days at the club, and Divine would have to compensate her for her losses. So when Divine asked Brooklyn how much money she would have made if she would've worked at the club, she told him anywhere between fifteen hundred and two thousand dollars. She stretched the truth a little, but fuck it, time was money, especially her time and Divine had plenty of it.

Brooklyn was dressed to impress. She had on her Coogi dress with some Chanel sandals that wrapped up around her calves. Her hair was wrapped in a style and in her ears were a pair of two carat princess cut, pink diamonds that her last man bought for her before he got locked up for life. Brooklyn wanted to impress Divine. Furthermore, she wanted some dick and if he acted right, he could be the one. It was already 11:25 and he hadn't shown up yet. She had paged him an hour ago. As soon as she started to get upset, she heard a car horn beeping. Brooklyn looked out her window and saw a 500 SL Benz sitting on spinning chrome. *Damn! This nigga is holding,* Brooklyn thought to herself. She yelled out the window that she was coming. "This nigga is balling more than I thought," Brooklyn said to herself as she snatched her keys and purse and was out the door.

As Brooklyn got into the car, Divine was on his cell phone. She gave Divine a kiss on his cheek and made a smacking sound just in case he was talking to a chick on the other line. Once Brooklyn got in, Divine hung the phone up. She wanted them to know that he was with someone else.

"Hey, what's up, boo? You're looking real good," Divine

said as he returned Brooklyn's kiss.

"What's up, Divine?" Brooklyn said as she admired the fine looking man.

Divine was light skinned with brown eyes and long corn-rolls going to the back. He had a sharp edge up that would cut you. Divine was 5'9" and 205 pounds of muscle. Divine was twenty-two years old and was only home a couple of months from federal prison. While he was in prison, he hooked up with a Columbian who was doing life. Divine shared a cell with him for four years. Within this time, he and Eneresto became real close. Divine put some work in on one of the rats that had snitched on Eneresto's case. Eneresto knew that Divine was soon to be released and he knew that Divine was a soldier, so he told Divine as soon as he's released to get in touch with his brother and he would take care of him. Eneresto's brother was in Miami. That's how Divine came up so quick. Eneresto's brother gave Divine 100 keys on consignment for 5 g's a brick. Within two weeks, Divine was back to see Raul with his money.

Raul was impressed with Divine. He gave Divine 200 keys at 4.5. Divine sold them in the hood at 16 a pop, but for his real playas, he gave it to them at 9.5. He still made a profit and they had to buy at least 10 or better. Off of the 200, he would make 1.1 mil and 900 would go to Raul. This was a come up for a nigga straight out of the system. Divine had a couple of people who copped like Big Ben did. He had one of his main mans that he had grown up with that hustled in Harlem named Mo'Better. Mo'Better moved about five a week. So as soon as he got shit from Raul, shit was movin', not to mention the locals from around the way he gave consignment to. Divine had damn near the whole Bedstuy working his shit. Divine had a mean team of s1's running and ready to lay their life on the line for him. He had it all, and the only thing missing was the right shorty. With the right shorty, Divine felt he could rule Brooklyn. And it was something about Brooklyn that attracted Divine besides her fat ass and good looks. He had to have her.

"Divine, what's on your mind that got you so deep in thought?" Brooklyn asked as she hit Divine on the arm to break his train of thought.

"Oh, pardon me, Boo, I was just calculating some figures in my head."

"Oh, you holding like that, huh?" She gave Divine a look that said, "Let me find out."

"Nah, ma, I just got to make sure my shit is right, that's all," Divine said and pulled off.

• • •

Diamond placed the suitcase in the baggage department on the bus and took a seat next to a window. She put on her Alicia Keys CD and laid back. She had a long ride, but fuck it, she had 5 g's in her pocket. She didn't care how long she had to ride on the bus. At least that mutha fucka was good for something because the dick and his head game was some trash. Diamond's thoughts were interrupted by a lady and her daughter sitting next to her. This was a good thing because she would act as if she was traveling with them.

• • •

Pop watched as Ben pulled off with Diamond. As soon as they turned the corner, he looked up at Diamond's window and Angel was waving for him to come upstairs. Diamond didn't know it but Angel had been getting high ever since the ordeal with Rahmel. And just recently, Angel started fucking Pop to support her habit. But she only used when Diamond wasn't around. She made it her business to never let Diamond find out.

When Pop entered the apartment, all Angel had on was her bra and a pair of Diamond's thongs.

"Yo, what's up, Angel? I see you let your daughter still run around with that nigga, huh?" Pop said as he sat on the couch.

"Pop, I have twenty-five dollars towards what I owe you, but I still need something. Can you help me?"

"Come on, how you trying to pay me what you owe but still want something?" Pop said as he grabbed his dick.

"We can work something out," Angel said as she licked her lips. "Did you put the police lock on just in case my daughter comes back?"

"Yeah, you know I know how this go, now come on, I don't have all day," Pop said as he dropped his pants.

Angel got on her knees, knelt between Pop's legs and began stroking his manhood until he stood at attention. She started sucking and licking on the knob of his cock as she stroked his shaft. Pop grabbed Angel by her long straight black hair and jammed his dick all the way into her mouth causing her to gag. As Angel gagged and choked on Pop's cock, he continued to fuck Angel's mouth as if he was fucking some pussy until he came. Pop then told Angel if she wanted the biggest rock he had that she would have to swallow every drop of his cum. Angel was reluctant at first, but the crave for the drug was much stronger than her will. Angel prayed that Diamond would never find out what she did when she wasn't around. Diamond had already been through a lot without her being disgraced by what her mother did to get high. But Angel knew it was only a matter of time.

Chapter 3
A Quick Come Up

When the bus pulled into the station, Diamond spotted Ben's Lexus parked but she didn't see Ben. As soon as Diamond stepped off the bus, a lady that was the spitting image of Ben stepped to her and said that Ben had sent her.

"Hi, my name is Pat, I'm Ben's aunt," the giant of a lady said as she helped Diamond with her bags.

Pat pulled into a block that was filled with one-story houses that were all built close together. If one was to catch fire, they all would burn down. It seemed as if every other house was boarded up. You could tell it was the hood part of N.C. When they walked into the house, there were about five obese kids at the table eating pig's feet. Diamond had never eaten pork in her life. Rahmel didn't allow it. As soon as the fumes from the pork hit her, she started feeling woozy. Pat led Diamond to the back room where Ben was with about five other younger looking dudes. When they walked into the room, nobody spoke as Ben took the bag from Diamond and started dividing the product between the occupants of the room. They all tested the work and were satisfied with the grain of coke. Ben had sold each package for 23.5 making a total of 117.5 easy. *As soon as*

I get back I'll hit that nigga vine off with his money first, Ben thought to himself. The price for coke was so high out there, so him having New York prices, he could corner the market in N.C. They were paying 30 and better for one. So if he sold his for 23.5, he'd make 14 on each which was a come up, because in New York he would only have made about four or five on each. He was gonna love that down-south money. His cousin wasn't lying.

"Yo, Ben, when are you coming back? Because I should be finished this in about two days," a short stocky dude with a mouthful of gold teeth said.

"Yo, whenever y'all need to see me, all y'all have to do is get with Forrest a day in advance. He'll get at me and I'll be here the next day. That's why I say to get in touch with him ahead of time." Ben was sitting a the table counting his money.

"Ben, if this shit is like you say it is, I'll be getting right back at you. I'ma just cop this one to test it," a tall cat who called himself Gangsta said.

When Ben first told Forrest that he wanted to bring some weight out there to sell, Forrest told Ben that he knew all the high rollers that were out there and that he'd let them know whenever he was ready. Forrest said that if he had shit from New York with the same prices, he'd make a killing out there. Because everybody wanted to get their work from New York, but didn't want to risk driving with all that shit in their cars or risk getting set up. So if they didn't have to travel to N.Y. and still got the same product for the same prices, they were with that one hundred percent.

After all the money was counted and the work was exchanged, everybody left. Ben no longer felt comfortable while he had all that money on him. He wanted to be out of N.C. as fast as he could. He looked at Diamond and knew that she didn't want to be there. She wasn't comfortable because she didn't know anybody. When Ben looked at Diamond, his dick got hard. He wanted to fuck, but he also wanted to get out of Dodge with all that money and back to New York.

"Yo, Diamond, come on, we're not staying. We're driving back tonight," Ben said as he neatly packed the money in the suitcase that Diamond came with.

Ben gave Forrest a kilo on consignment.

"Yo, Forrest, don't fuck that money up, son. If you do it right, there's plenty more where that came from," Ben told his cousin as he gave him a pound.

Forrest planned on bagging up the whole cake into 20 dollar pieces. He would get close to 50 g's off of one cake. That was enough for him to trick on some stripper broads and enough to pay Ben.

"Aight, big cuz, I got you. Don't worry about it. I got this. You act like I'm a busta or something. I just made you over a hundred g's, nigga, damn! Yo, cuz, what's up with your shorty. She's fine. You know it ain't no fun unless little cuz get some," Forrest said as he walked Ben and Diamond to the car.

Diamond felt relieved that she wouldn't have to stay the night with Ben. She wasn't trying to fuck him any more. The next time Ben wanted some pussy, she would use cramps as an excuse not to fuck. She had enough money to last her and if he wanted her to make another run for him, he would have to pay her more money. Because her life was on the line riding with all them drugs in that bag. The money was good, but fuck that—it wasn't worth her doing life in prison.

As soon as Diamond got in the car, she reclined her seat back and closed her eyes. Diamond could feel Ben rubbing on her thigh as he drove, but she ignored him. Diamond's thoughts were on Shymeek.

• • •

Shymeek was in Atlanta working on one of the local rap artist's albums who was getting a big buzz in Atlanta. Shymeek was twenty-six years old and an up and coming producer. He did beats for many of the newest artists and recently he had signed to a major label. Shymeek had partied for the last two days. Everyday was a party in Atlanta, everyday a different strip club. But for some reason, he couldn't get this young pretty thing he had met in Brooklyn a couple of weeks ago out of his mind. They had spoken a couple of times, but he had yet to spend time with her. Today was Diamond's birthday and he wanted to be with her. He had the perfect gift to get her so he could impress her. Shymeek knew that Diamond was young, but he was turned on by her realness and her conversation intrigued him. She was definitely a jewel.

Shymeek was snapped out of his thoughts of Diamond when his engineer asked him to retake the last fifteen bars of the track and re-loop the break.

"Yo, son, take it from the beginning and ad lib your vocals," Shymeek said to the MC.

Shymeek's mind wasn't on his work. He couldn't understand why he couldn't get Diamond out of his head. After the session, he would take a couple of days off. That was one of the good things about being a producer—you dictate your own work schedule. Shymeek was going back to Brooklyn for a couple of days. All he needed the MC to do was lay his lyrics and he could lay the beat around his vocals. After the session, Shymeek would tell his engineer that their next studio session would be the following week on Sunday. Shymeek went back to his hotel, packed his suitcase and jumped into a cab to the airport.

• • •

After Divine and Brooklyn finished their meal at Juniors, he drove to the piers in Canarsie. They sat and talked for about an hour. Brooklyn was surprised. Divine had given her a G to take the night off from dancing and to spend the night with him. Brooklyn just knew he was gonna want some pussy and she was willing to give it to him.

Divine pulled into the pier and parked his luxury car facing the water. They reclined their seats back and rolled a blunt of the chronic, while Mario Winans' CD was playing.

"Brooklyn, I'm feelin' you as you can see. I want you mentally, emotionally and physically, but I don't want you to think that all I want you for is your sex. I like the way you carry yourself. I need a girl who is willing to troop with me through thick and thin. I know we just met, but to me, that was enough time for me to see something in you that attracted me to you," Divine said as he looked into Brooklyn's eyes and passed her the blunt to light.

"Divine, please, I would love to be with you, but I know you're doing your thing out there," Brooklyn said as she lit the blunt.

"Listen, Brooklyn, if I was trying to game you, I wouldn't even be here. I'm not going to lie to you and tell you I wasn't fucking somebody. I am a man who not too long ago just came home from prison. But what I am telling you is that I'm feeling you and if this is right, let's make it happen. I can also tell you this. If you was my girl, you'd never have to strip or dance in nobody's club or work again."

"Yeah, that sounds good, Divine, but what happens if you decide to get somebody else?"

"Hold up, boo. All that would depend on you and I. We are the creators of our own destiny. It's all about how we connect.

If this was meant to be, then all things would come into play. Listen, just give this a chance. What you think?" he asked sincerely.

"Believe me, Divine, that sounds real good, but you must understand how I feel. It's hard for me to believe. All my life I had it hard and out of nowhere, here comes my prince charming to snatch me up. You must say, this is some fairy tale shit for a girl like me who never had anything. So what do you want me to say?" Brooklyn asked as she reclined her seat back and let the effects of the get high, music and Divine cultivate her thoughts.

Brooklyn was feelin' Divine. She was in the mood to fuck and everything about Divine was turning her on.

He looked over at her. "What's up, Brooklyn? What are you thinking about?"

"You." She kept her eyes closed but smiled anyway.

"I hope it's something good," Divine was leaned up on one elbow admiring Brooklyn's beauty.

"That all depends!" she giggled a little bit.

"Depends on what?" Divine was really smiling now.

"You."

"Oh, here we go again with the one word answers."

As soon as the last words left Divine's mouth, Brooklyn leaned over and pulled Divine's face to hers and stuck her tongue in his mouth. As Divine slowly kissed Brooklyn, he put his hand up her dress, pulled her panties to the side and started finger poppin' and playing with Brooklyn's clit until she came. As Brooklyn laid back in the chair and started shaking and convulsing from her orgasm, Divine thought to himself how tight Brooklyn's pussy felt. Divine could imagine how she would react to the dick if she was cumming off of his finger. What would happen if he laid the pipe to her. Divine's dick got hard just thinking about making love to Brooklyn. Divine pulled his finger out of Brooklyn, licked it and savored the taste. He couldn't wait to lick her from head to toe. Brooklyn was turned on by Divine licking her pussy juices off of his finger. She wanted to pleasure him beyond comprehension. She whispered in his ear to drive as Brooklyn unzipped Divine's pants and proceeded to give him some head. Divine wanted to close his eyes as he felt Brooklyn's lips wrap around the head of his cock. Divine tried his best not to crash his eighty thousand dollar car. Brooklyn was working him so good that he had to pull over. As he was pulling off the road, he was cumming. Brooklyn told Divine that she wanted him right there in the car. Divine reclined his seat back as far as it would go and he pulled his pants down to his ankles. Brooklyn pulled her skirt up, pulled her panties off and then straddled Divine. Brooklyn laid back on the steering wheel and used her hands to support her weight on Divine's thighs as he sucked on her breast and rammed his cock into her in an upward motion. She bounced on his cock with every thrust. Within five minutes, they both were at the point of climax. The excitement of cars driving by seeing them make love made their sexcapade that more pleasurable and exciting. Before they knew it, they both were cumming simultaneously.

"Damn, boo! I never did that before," Divine explained.

"Me neither. You just got my pussy's juices flowing and I needed to have you," Brooklyn said as she fixed her clothes.

"Man! If it was like that in the car, I can't wait to get you in the bed."

"Then what's the hold up. Let's go, Daddy," she said straightening out her skirt.

"You ain't said nothing but a word. Let's go." Divine put the car in *drive* and took off.

• • •

As soon as Angel finished smoking the last of her rock, she immediately felt guilty. Every ten minutes she thought that she heard keys turning in the door. Angel knew if Diamond knew what she was doing, she would be crushed. Diamond was all Angel had and she didn't want to lose her because she was weak. Angel reflected on the events of her life and started crying. Rahmel had destroyed her. Now she had started sobering up to the reality that she didn't do anything that she was supposed to do. The money was gone and she had let Pop fuck her and disrespect her and her body. Angel blamed all of her troubles on Rahmel.

• • •

When Ben and Diamond pulled up to her block, Pop and his crew were all standing in front of the corner store as usual. Ben was tired from the round trip to N.C. and back. He was beat. Diamond had slept the whole ride back. He woke Diamond up and let her know that they were back.

"Yo, Diamond, we're in front of your building," he said shaking her leg.

"Damn, that was fast!" Diamond said as she stretched. She looked around.

"Fast! I've been driving for hours. Listen, as soon as these cats call me, I'ma need you to make this move again for me, ya heard?"

"Yeah, I hear you, but I'ma need more than what you gave me this time because it's too big of a risk with all that shit you gave me. I'm not trying to go to jail."

"We'll talk about that," Ben said as Diamond got out the car.

As Ben pulled off, he stopped at the red light and he once

again noticed Pop and his crew staring at him. The light turned green and Ben turned the system up and pulled off.

When Diamond walked into the apartment, all the lights were off and the TV was on. Angel was knocked out on the couch. Diamond gave her moms a kiss, turned the TV off and went to bed. Tomorrow, she and Angel would go shopping and get their hair and nails done. It was time for her mother to get on with her life and stop stressing over things over which she had no power. Angel was still young and pretty, so Diamond planned on giving her mother a makeover so Angel could start dating again and find herself a new man.

Chapter 4

One More Time

Diamond slept for close to fourteen straight hours and her pager was ringing off the hook. It was 10 a.m. Big Ben had dropped her off at 8 p.m. the night before. Diamond looked at her pager. She had nine pages; five of them were from Ben, two were from Brooklyn and two other numbers she didn't recognize. This was odd because Brooklyn and Ben were the only ones who had the number. She figured it was Ben calling from another number. But her curiosity got the best of her, so she immediately called the last two numbers back.

"Did somebody page Diamond?"

"Yo, what's up, shorty? You act like you don't know how to get at a brother!"

"Who's this?" Diamond asked, already knowing who it was.

"Who do you want it to be? You have that many dudes paging you where it's hard for you to keep up?"

"That's the problem. I didn't give anybody my number! But I know who this is."

"A brother got his ways of getting your number. Was it a problem?"

"No, it wasn't. I'm glad you did. Of course, I was gonna call you. I just got up. You caught me by surprise when I heard your voice," Diamond said, as she tried to hold back the excitement of hearing Shymeek's voice.

"What 'cha doing today? I'm trying to get with you," Shymeek said as he guided his Range Rover through traffic.

"My mother and I are going to get our hair and nails done at the mall downtown."

"As soon as you finish, give me a ring. Call the number that's on your pager. That's my cell phone, aight?"

"I have a better idea. Meet me downtown so I can introduce you to my moms. Aight, I'll be waitin'."

"Aight, I'll see you around 3 or 4. Peace!"

As soon as Diamond got off the phone, she went to check to see if the house phone was on and if her mother bought any food for the house. The phone was still off and there was no food in the fridge. Diamond went into the living room and Angel was laid out as if she had partied all day and night.

"Ma. Ma, come one, get up. Ma, come on, get up." Diamond had to shake Angel a couple of times before she got up.

"Diamond! When did you get back?" Angel asked as she looked at the clock on the wall.

"I came back around 8 o'clock last night, and you was out cold on the couch. Ma, why didn't you go pay the phone bill or go get some food for the house?" Diamond put her hands on her sides.

"I got to the phone company too late. I'ma have to go on Monday. And I was too tired to go to the market."

"Listen, we're going to go out and do a little one on one. Just you and me. Go get all pretty so we can knock 'em dead when we go to the club tonight. It's time for you to live a little."

"Girl, where are you getting all of this money from?" Angel asked with concern in her voice.

"Ma, you know Ben gives me money." She walked into her room.

"Diamond, I hope you're not doing anything illegal with that boy. You're all that I have and if anything happened to you, I'd be no more good."

"Ma, don't even worry about that. Don't you think I know better? You just hurry up so we can go spend some of Ben's money."

As Angel got up to take a shower, guilt started to kick in about the events of her secrets for the last couple of months; her down low life. She knew that she couldn't do much for Diamond because she was fucked up herself. Right then she had made the decision to go cold turkey. Diamond meant too much to her to lose her because of her sickness. It was time to get her life together and stop blaming herself for the hell that Rahmel put her through. "I'm thirty-three years old and looking like I'm fifty. Walking around this apartment killing myself in my own misery. I still have a lot of living to do, if not for me, for Diamond," Angel said to herself as she jumped into the shower. She would sit Diamond down and tell her of her addiction and pray that she would understand. Come Monday morning, she would go check herself into a detox center and sign up for a rehab.

Diamond called Brooklyn's house and Brooklyn's aunt told her that Brooklyn left with a dude in a Benz the night before and had yet to return. Diamond figured who Brooklyn went out with, then she called Big Ben back.

"Ben, what's up?" she said not really giving a damn.

"Yo, Diamond, where have you been? I've been trying to

reach you since last night." Ben looked at his watch.

"I just got up. As soon as you dropped me off, I fell out and didn't get up until just now."

"Listen, I need you to make another move with me tonight. What are you doing right now?"

"I'm about to go get my hair and my nails done with my mother, and then we're going shopping."

"As soon as you finish, I need you to get in touch with me because I need you bad. The boys from down south called me last night. They need to see me like yesterday. 911! A lot of money is riding on this trip. I need you. Please don't let me down."

"Ben, you remember what I told you about paying me right?"

"Don't worry about that, Diamond. You know I got you. I'ma take care of you. Trust me. Off of this I'ma eat real good, or should I say, we're going to eat real good. You know that I'm going to make sure you're alright." He smiled to himself as he thought about his other family.

"Alright, Ben, I should be finished around nine and I'll see you around ten tonight. Aight, and have everything ready so I can just get on the bus. Oh yeah, I'm not trying to stay because my friend came and I'm not feelin' well." Diamond threw that in there just in case Ben wanted some pussy. She wasn't trying to fuck with him like that anymore. She had enough money so to her, their sexcapades were over. She didn't wanna have sex with him anymore, but she liked the money.

As soon as she hung the phone up, she remembered that she had promised Shymeek that they would hook up. She was feelin' Shymeek but she needed the money that Ben paid her for transporting his drugs to N.C. for him. "Maybe after we get our hair done I'll spend some time with Shymeek then hook up with Ben," Diamond said to herself as she looked out the window.

Damn! These niggas never go in. They stand on the corners all night and day. And they're still broke, she thought to herself.

While Diamond and Angel walked to the train station, Rahmel drove by in a brand new Benz with a girl who looked to be about sixteen years old. "Ma, look!" Diamond said as she pointed to her father.

"I hope that mutha fucka didn't see us. Look at him riding around in a brand new car and we're starving," Angel said with hatred in her voice.

"Ma, don't stress that no good mutha fucka. He was too into that little girl he was with to notice us. Stop worrying about that nigga. We're doing better without him. We'll survive. Just me and you," Diamond said as she hugged her mother before they went into the train station.

• • •

Divine took Brooklyn to the Marriott Hotel and made love to her all night. Divine's mind was made up. Brooklyn was going to be his main girl. He was gonna bless her and get her right. He had big plans for her.

While they both laid in the bed smoking a blunt and enjoying each other's company, Divine's pager went off. Divine grabbed his two-way out of his pant's pocket that was laying on the floor next to the bed. It was Big Ben.

Damn! That big nigga is doing his thing, Divine thought to himself. He called Big Ben back. As Divine dialed his cell phone, Brooklyn began giving him some *hot jaw.* Divine closed his eyes and enjoyed Brooklyn's work.

"Ahh! Oh, yo, you paged me?" Divine said into the phone

trying to hold back his moans from the deep throat Brooklyn was giving him.

"Vine, this is Ben. I need to see you like 911. Ya heard?" Ben said as he heard the slurping sounds of Divine getting head. "Yo, boy, what are you doing? It sounds like you're getting your man ate up."

"Yo son, I'll hit you back in 30, once I get back to the spot, ahight." Divine responded before he quickly hung up the phone and returned his focus back on Brooklyn giving him the monster brain.

"Ohhh, yes, work it! Yes! Work that dick, shorty, yes! Yeah, right there, Brooklyn, right there!" Divine moaned as Brooklyn bounced her head up and down taking all of Divine's manhood. When she felt his cock start to stiffen up, Brooklyn climbed on top of him and started bouncing up and down on his hard shaft. Divine laid back while he rubbed and squeezed Brooklyn's firm chest while she worked her magic. Divine knew he couldn't hold back any longer. He grabbed hold of Brooklyn's hips so he could dig deep and touch every inch of her walls as he filled her insides with his cum. As Brooklyn rolled over in ecstasy, she thought about what just happened.

"Divine, why'd you do that?" she had a serious look on her face.

"Why'd I do what?" Divine was laying on his side caressing Brooklyn's plump ass.

"You know what I'm talking about." She looked at him.

"No, I don't, tell me. You didn't enjoy yourself?" Divine sat up on one elbow.

"Boy! Of course I enjoyed myself, and you know good and damn well that I wasn't talking about that. I'm talking about you cumming inside of me. Why didn't you pull out?"

"Oh, that's what you're talking about," Divine said as he

laughed.

"Oh, that shit is funny to you, huh? Divine, I'm not ready to get pregnant. I already have a son that my grandmother takes care of."

"Stop worrying. You're not going to get pregnant. But I couldn't help myself. It was feeling too good to a nigga to pull out. I got caught up," Divine said as Brooklyn tried to get up to go wash up. Divine pulled her back down on top of him and gave her a passionate kiss and started sucking on her chest. She felt Divine growing erect again.

"Listen, Brooklyn, I want you to be my girl. I believe with you at my side, I could rule the world. Let me take you away from all the bullshit, Brooklyn. Fuck all that stripping shit. You can own a strip club if that's what you want."

Before Brooklyn could say anything, Divine put his index finger on her lips stopping her from speaking and went down on her.

• • •

As Diamond and Angel sat under the hair dryer in the beauty salon at the ground level of the mall, an all-white Range Rover pulled up in front. When the Range came to a complete stop, the twenty-four inches of chrome wheels kept spinning. It was kind of hypnotizing. Diamond watched with excitement as Shymeek jumped out of the Range wearing a brand new pair of all-white *uptowns* with a fresh pair of Sean John black velour sweatpants and a wife beater showing his well toned body. Shymeek had on enough jewelry to bring down the temperature outside. He had on a platinum bracelet that was flooded with black diamonds. On his other wrist he had the platinum Presidential Rolex with the iced out bezel. The shop became quiet when he entered the salon. All eyes were on him.

Diamond felt kinda special that this God's gift to women was coming to see her. When Shymeek entered with a dozen of long stem roses and a box, you could hear all the ladies' in the salon hearts stop. Even Angel was taken by this handsome man. Shymeek walked over to Diamond, gave her a kiss and handed her the flowers.

"What's up, boo? I bought you a little something, a late birthday gift," Shymeek said as he handed Diamond the small box he had in his hand.

"Shymeek, this is my mother," Diamond said accepting her gift and introducing Shymeek to her mother.

"Your who? Your mother, where?" Shymeek said not believing Angel was her mother.

"Yes, I am Diamond's mother and how are you?" Angel said as she shook Shymeek's hand.

"Oh, excuse me, Mrs. Angel, I'm not trying to be rude, but you could pass for her sister. You don't look a day over twenty-five. Now I see where she got her beauty," Shymeek said accepting her hand and kissing the back of it.

Angel blushed from the compliment and responded, "Well, I'm not too far from twenty-five. I had Diamond when I was young."

Diamond opened her gift and pulled out a platinum bracelet with her name in diamonds. She jumped out of her chair and hugged Shymeek and stuck her tongue down his throat.

"Shymeek, thank you." Her smile was almost as bright as the stones in her bracelet.

"Do you like it?" Shymeek asked, knowing damn well that she did.

"Yes! Oh, yes, I love it." She was fingering the merchandise.

"How much longer do y'all have? Because I want to take y'all out to eat."

"Another fifteen minutes and we're finished."

"Aight, I'ma wait in the car. I have a few phone calls to make," Shymeek said. He turned around and walked out of the salon.

As soon as Shymeek left the salon, Angel started questioning Diamond about Shymeek.

"Where did you meet him and how old is he?"

"I met Shymeek at a club when I was out with Brooklyn a few weeks ago. And if you need to know, Miss Thing, he's eighteen," Diamond said feeling bad that she lied to her mother, but she knew if she told Angel his true age she wouldn't approve. Angel wanted Diamond to date guys that were her age, but Diamond felt that guys her age were too immature.

"Diamond, why are all these guys giving you all of these expensive gifts and money? Girl, I bet not find out that you're out there doing anything illegal," Angel said having an idea that when Diamond goes out of town with Ben and returns the next day that she's transporting drugs for him. She knew because that was what she used to do for Rahmel before she had Diamond.

"Ma, please, must we go through this again?"

"Diamond, I don't want anything happening to you. Dealing with men like that, that's in the game, nothing good ever comes out of that. Look at me and your father's situation." Angel rolled her eyes.

"Ma, Shymeek is a music producer. He makes records," Diamond said as she paid for her and her mother's bill.

As they left the salon, Diamond could feel the hate that was coming from the women that were in the salon. They jumped into the Range Rover and Shymeek took them to

Juniors for dinner and cheesecake. They all sat, ate and talked until 9:30. Shymeek had some business to attend to, so he asked Diamond could he see her the next day. Diamond told him that it would be better for them to get together the following day because she had something extremely important to do. "So it's a date then," Shymeek said. He paid for the check as they prepared to leave.

Shymeek dropped them off at home and as soon as Diamond got upstairs, she called Big Ben.

• • •

Once Divine dropped Brooklyn off at her house, he called Big Ben back and told him to meet him at the spot.

When Divine pulled up to the building, Big Ben was sitting in his car parked across the street from the building with a crackhead bitch in the front seat with him. Divine got out of his car and motioned for Ben to come on. Divine whispered something in the ear of one of his runners who was standing out front. He threw him the keys to his Benz. Divine entered the building with Ben close behind him as Divine's runner pulled off.

Divine took Ben to a different apartment than before. They went into the basement of an apartment that was in the back of the boiler room. This was the stash apartment where some of the drugs were kept. Ben counted out the money he owed Divine from the 5 he got on consignment and then he counted out 47.5 and asked Divine could he give him 5 more at the same price.

"Yo, Ben, you know how I do. You have to buy at least 10 to get 'em at that price, son," Divine said as he counted the money Big Ben gave him.

"Yeah, Vine, I know, but I got these cats down south that

are sitting on a gold mine. I still have about 6 of my own left. But these cats want 10. As soon as I get it, I promise I'ma see you big. That's my word. Just let me get them 5 for the 9.5 a piece. Word on my life, Vine. I got you."

"Ben, I got you man, but don't make this shit a habit, son. Yo, you got yourself a gold mine down there, huh?"

"Yeah, them country boys know how to get that money. Ya heard?"

"Yeah, but you have to be careful with them niggas because they don't like niggas from New York. They'll set you up or tell on a nigga quick out there. I was locked up with them niggas for years. They can't stand us, son. For real," Divine said as his man gave him his car keys that was coming into the apartment.

"Yo, Ben, you met my little man, Meth, already, right?" Divine asked Ben as Meth gave him a box of blunts and a bottle of Henny.

"Yeah, I met him the last time," Ben said giving Meth a head nod.

"Yo, Meth, get Ben 5 of them things for me."

As soon as Meth left the room, Ben started explaining how he operated in N.C.

"Vine, I know how them niggas get down out there, but it ain't like that with the cats that I fuck with. I got a lot of family out there and they know I'm not trying to just fuck with anybody."

"Oh, aight, son, that's good because them niggas out there are snakes," Divine said as Meth entered the room with a Jan sports bag.

Meth put the 5 keys on the table.

"Yo, Vine, if that is the same shit as before, I don't have to test it."

"You don't ever have to worry about me giving you some garbage, son."

"I know, son," Ben said as he packed the keys back into the Jan sports bag. Ben gave Divine a pound and Meth a head nod as he left the apartment. He got into the car and passed the bag to the fiend and pulled off. Ben called Diamond and told her to meet him downstairs in fifteen minutes.

Chapter 5
When An Angel Falls

Diamond had finally caught up with Brooklyn. She told her of the little move she made to N.C. for Big Ben and how he gave her 5 g's and that she was going again that evening. Brooklyn didn't agree with Diamond going back to back on the Greyhound with drugs to North Carolina. But she knew Diamond was gonna do it anyway. She knew that she and her mother had it kinda bad lately and that they needed the money. Diamond told her about the gift Shymeek had bought her and about how he made a grand entrance at the salon with a dozen white long stem roses and how he took her and Angel out to eat. Of course, Brooklyn shoved her sex fest with Divine down Diamond's throat and how Divine gave her a G just to chill with him. Also that Divine was her new man now. While they spoke, Big Ben had beeped in and told Diamond to be outside in fifteen minutes, that he was on his way.

As soon as Diamond got off the phone with Brooklyn, she went into the living room with her mother. Diamond explained to her mother why Big Ben had given her so much money. Diamond told Angel everything about her going to N.C. and that she would be on her way back that evening. Angel was disappointed but with the guilt from her smoking, there wasn't much she could say or do. Diamond went into her room and stashed her money in her mattress. In all, including the 4500 she had left from the 5 g's, she had saved a total of six thousand dollars. While she was stashing her money, she heard Ben's horn blowing.

"Damn, this fat mutha fucka is gonna be pissed that I wasn't downstairs. He acts as if he's scared of these niggas around here," Diamond said to herself as she left the room.

"Ma, Ben is here. I'm gone. I'll be back tomorrow."

"Baby, please be careful," Angel said as she hugged Diamond.

Diamond told her mother not to worry, that everything was going to be okay. She gave Angel a hundred dollars and left. As soon as Diamond left the house, Angel's addiction started to kick in.

"I can't do this anymore. Today is the last time. After this $100, I'm checking myself into rehab, first thing Monday morning," Angel said to herself.

Angel watched Ben pull off and she flagged Pop to come up.

• • •

Pop and his man Regg were on the corner smoking dust, getting wet. As soon as Ben pulled up in front of Diamond's crib, Pop tapped his man on the shoulder and pointed to Ben's Lexus.

"Look, son, there go that fat mutha fucka again. Yo, we got to get that nigga one of these days," Pop said to his man as he looked up and noticed Angel in her window trying to get his attention.

"Yo, son, you wanna go hit that fat ass? We better dog it

out now before she get on this shit. *And* she sucks a mean dick. Ya heard? Come on, let's go."

Pop and his man went upstairs to Angel's apartment.

"Come in, the door is open."

"Yo, what's up, Angel. I brought my little man with me," Pop said as he sat on the couch. "A yo, Angel. Me and my little man want you to show us a good time," Pop said as he pulled out five 20 pieces of rock.

"Oh, nah, Pop. I have money and today is my last time. I'm going into rehab. I'm trying to get my life right."

"Hold up, bitch. What are you talking about. You still owe me from the last time."

"I know, Pop, I got your money," Angel said as she pulled out one hundred dollars.

"Bitch, we don't want no money. We want our dicks sucked," Pop said as he grabbed Angel by the neck and pulled his dick out.

"Oh, no, boy, don't be putting your fucking hands on me," Angel said as she tried to pull Pop's hands from off her neck.

"Bitch!"

Smack!!!

Once Angel fell, Pop and Regg started punching and stomping on Angel's head. Angel lost consciousness. Pop pulled down Angel's pants while she was unconscious and started fucking her.

"Yo, son, what are you doing? Yo, she's fucked up, son. We probably killed her. Come on, son. What are you doing? This shit is rape," Regg said as he pulled on Pop's arm to try and stop him from raping Angel.

"Man, fuck this crackhead bitch! I'ma get my man off," Pop said as he continued to rape and sodomize Angel while she was unconscious.

"Yo, son, I'm not with this," Regg said as he ran out of the apartment.

As Pop stayed in the apartment and continued to rape Angel, he fantasized that she was Diamond.

"Yeah, you little bitch, you wanna ride around with that fat nigga but don't wanna give me a play. Take this, bitch. Uhh!! Yeah, bitch, how do you like it in the ass, hoe? Uhh, yeah, yeah, uhh, you stinking bitch," Pop said as he fucked Angel recklessly. He was feeling the effects of the angel dust.

As soon as Pop came, he got up, kicked Angel in the face, threw some crack on the floor and walked out the door.

• • •

Brooklyn laid in her bed thinking about the fucking that Divine had put on her the night before. She had promised Divine that her dancing days were over. She wondered how serious he was about making her his girl. *Divine had plenty of money and could have any girl he wanted.* Brooklyn's thought was interrupted by a knock on the door.

"Who is it?" she asked.

"Delivery."

She squenched up her face because she wasn't expecting anything. Brooklyn opened the door and spotted a man standing with a UPS suit on with a small box and a clipboard in his hand.

"Excuse me, I have a package for a Brooklyn from a Divine."

"Yes, that's me," she said happily.

The UPS man gave Brooklyn his clipboard and a pen to sign. As soon as she signed it, he handed her the package. Brooklyn closed the door and ripped into the package.

"Oh, my God! Oh, my God!" she screamed hysterically.

Brooklyn's aunt came out of the kitchen to see what her niece was screaming about.

"Girl, what's wrong with you?" her aunt asked.

"Look what Divine just sent me."

Brooklyn pulled out the two carat Jacob and Co. Evil Eye bracelet.

"Oh, shit, girl, that nigga really wants you. This bracelet costs about ten thousand dollars," Brooklyn's aunt said as she helped her put it on her wrist.

As soon as she put the bracelet on, she called Divine.

"Divine, thank you so much."

"How much are you thankful?" Divine asked as he thought about the fucking Brooklyn had put on him the night before. "Are you thankful enough to jump in a cab right now and come to Queens?"

"I'll be there. Just give me the address and thirty minutes."

After Brooklyn wrote down the address, she hung up the phone and called a cab.

• • •

As soon as Diamond pulled into the station, Ben and Forrest were waiting in Ben's car. Forrest got out of the car and helped Diamond with her bags.

"How was your trip, Diamond?" Ben asked as he pulled off.

"Long and boring, but for the money you gave me, fuck it." She rested her head on the headrest.

"Listen, we're not going to the house. We're going to meet up with Forrest's man, and then we're gonna drop Forrest off and go to a hotel. Aight?" Ben said as he turned on 50 Cents' *Get Rich or Die Trying* C.D. It was Big Ben's theme music.

Twenty minutes later they were pulling off a dirt road into

what appeared to be some sort of warehouse or factory. Ben told Diamond to lay down in the back because Forrest told Ben that the dude wouldn't deal if he knew they had somebody with them.

"Yo, Forrest, I'm not feelin' this, son," Ben said as he looked at his cousin for reassurance. "Why I never met this cat?" Ben asked.

"He just came home. Man, don't worry about it. He's cool. Trust me," Forrest said getting out of the car.

"Ben, if you're having bad vibes about this, let's leave," Diamond said from her bent over position in the back seat.

"Man, listen, cuz, this cat has over a hundred thousand and he wants to spend it with you. So let's get this money, man. He's aight," Forrest assured his cousin.

Ben pulled in front of a black Range Rover with two dudes in it dressed in black with a neck full of platinum on. One was short and stocky and the other, a tall slim cat with shades on. Ben didn't like the scene at all. Forrest got out of the car and walked up to the two dudes and gave them pounds.

"What's up, Forrest?" the tall slim cat with the glasses said.

"What's up, Slim? Was y'all here long waitin'?" Forrest asked as he waved Big Ben to get out of the car.

"Make sure you stay down," Ben told Diamond as he got out of the car with the suitcase of drugs.

Diamond was scared to death. She didn't like the fact that she had to hide in the back seat. *What if shit went down and these niggas come and checked the back seat out?* Diamond thought to herself. After this she wasn't ever doing this with Ben again. *Fuck the money.*

Bang! Bang! Bang!...Bang!

"Oh, my God." Diamond started shaking as she pissed on

herself.

Diamond said a silent prayer as she heard two car doors slam and the car speed away. "PLEASE, PLEASE, GOD, PLEASE." Diamond slowly peeped her head up and started shaking violently when she noticed Ben and Forrest laying on the floor. She looked around to see if the car was gone. Once she realized that the car was nowhere in sight, Diamond jumped out of the car and ran over to where Ben and Forrest lay in their own blood. Ben was dead with two gunshot wounds to his head and Forrest wasn't conscious, but he was still alive. Diamond immediately called 911 and scrambled through her pockets looking for Forrest's house number. Diamond noticed the suitcase of drugs was gone. Diamond couldn't find the number so she checked Ben's pockets. Ben had 10 G's in cash and a box with a three carat diamond ring in it with his aunt's number balled up in his small pocket. Diamond took the money and ring and called his aunt's house.

When the police came, they held Diamond for questioning for hours. She told them that she didn't know what was going on, that Ben was her boyfriend and that he asked her to come to N.C. with him for the weekend, and when they got there they met with Ben's cousin where they drove to meet some other guys. "I don't know and don't ask questions. I was just riding," Diamond said as she started crying. They released her and that's when she found out that Forrest had died as well. The police never checked her so she still had the five Ben gave her for the trip, plus the 10 and the ring she took off of Ben's dead body. It was too late to catch a bus back, so she would have to wait until 5 in the morning for the first bus or train leaving to New York. She refused to go to the Aunt's house so she took a cab to the hotel.

● ● ●

The cab pulled up in front of the address in Queens that Brooklyn was given. There were three luxury cars parked in front of a baby mansion.

Damn, this nigga is on top of his game, Brooklyn thought to herself when she noticed Divine come to the door with a silk Gucci robe on and mink slippers. Divine paid the cab and took Brooklyn on a grand tour of the house.

As soon as she entered the house, the first thing she noticed was the 500-gallon fish tank inside the wall with all types of exotic fish in it. All the furniture was black leather with gold trimming. On the opposite wall she noticed an emblem of a 7, a moon and a star that was black, gold and white. This was the same sign that she saw the wu-tang wearing, so she figured Divine to be a 5 percenter. There was a 70-inch flat screen TV with an entertainment system built around it with a CD player, DVD and surround sound stereo. He also had an all-black rug that felt as if you were walking on clouds when you stepped on it. In the middle of the black rug, stitched in gold, was the word "Divine." Brooklyn couldn't believe his bedroom. Divine had a bed the size of Shaq's bed that she saw on MTV Cribs. He had a mink bedspread and a mirror on his ceiling. The frame of the bed was brass with a flat screen TV that raised from the foot of the bed. Divine had the type of house that people saw on *MTV Cribs.* She couldn't believe that this young twenty-year-old was paid like this and he wanted her. In the middle of his bedroom, he had a Jacuzzi. Music came from the walls throughout the house. Over Divine's bed he had a painting of a woman holding a baby and a man standing over them. At the bottom of the painting was the saying "*As it is in Heaven, so shall it be on Earth.*"

Brooklyn noticed the Jacuzzi was filled with water and scented candles all around it. Divine dropped his robe on the floor and Brooklyn almost lost her breath to see Divine standing before her with his chiseled rock-hard body and his manhood standing at attention. Divine walked up to Brooklyn and started sucking on her neck.

"Are you ready to show me how thankful you are? Because I'm ready to show you how thankful I am to have you," Divine said as he slowly undressed Brooklyn.

As Divine unbuttoned her shirt, he sucked on Brooklyn's neck. Her neck was sensitive and Divine knew it. He pulled off her shirt and unhooked her bra. He licked and sucked on her nipples. Brooklyn moaned in ecstasy as she felt herself becoming wet from Divine's touch. She wanted him bad. Once he had her fully undressed, he led her to the Jacuzzi. When he entered into the water, he sat on the edge and placed her legs over his shoulders. Divine started licking on the inside of her thighs. Divine zeroed in on Brooklyn's clit and started licking and flipping it with the tip of his tongue. He grabbed her ass cheeks with each one of his hands, squeezed and parted her ass while he stuck his pointer finger in her anal tunnel. He sucked and licked every inch of her insides and sucked her clit until it was swollen. Brooklyn moaned and screamed until she couldn't take it anymore. Her legs locked up around Divine's neck when she started cumming. Divine centered his assault on the pussy with his mouth. Brooklyn came so hard that she became exhausted. Divine bent her over the edge of the Jacuzzi and ate her out from the back until she came again. He entered her while she was bent over and licked and sucked on her neck. He made slow circular motions, then hard and fast strokes trying to shift Brooklyn's vaginal walls. Brooklyn screamed with every stroke. The more she screamed, the harder and faster Divine thrust his strokes.

Once again, Divine came inside of Brooklyn. Brooklyn

had never experienced so many orgasms at one time. *Divine was the man for her,* she thought to herself as they both laid over the edge of the Jacuzzi in the same position in which they had fucked.

"Did you like that?" Divine whispered in her ear.

"Divine, I don't know why you're doing this to me," Brooklyn said as she lay in the water trying to relax herself. She was on cloud nine. Her vaginal walls were pulsating. He had put that thing on her.

"Hold up, Brooklyn, I'm just trying to bring you where you should be. You are a queen and you deserve the world. Everybody wants heaven and I believe you and I can achieve that," Divine said as he poured a glass of Crystal for both of them.

"Divine, why me?" she blushed and looked at him.

"Why not you? As soon as I saw you, Brooklyn, I felt your presence. I was locked up for five years and in the last couple of months, I'm not gonna lie to you, I've fucked a few chicks but not one of them made me feel the way I feel for you. I know a lot of dudes might think I'm crazy because I just met you and at a strip club at that, but only I know what my heart speaks. All my life I've been a pretty good judge of character and I feel you're the one for me," Divine said as he reached over and pulled out a ring box from the pocket of his robe.

Brooklyn covered her mouth with her hands. She couldn't believe what was happening to her. *Is this a dream?* she asked herself.

"Brooklyn, I want you to be with me forever. Please accept this ring and think about our future together," Divine said as he revealed a two carat pink diamond encased in a red gold band.

"Divine," Brooklyn said as she accepted the ring and

started crying, "how could you know that you would want to be with me? You just met me. Let's be real with each other," she said with tears in her eyes.

"Brooklyn, I'm not about any games. I have over a million dollars in cash, over a million in cars and property. I had all of this in a matter of months, and I have no children. I want to share what I have accomplished with a family. We can grow together. I'm a strong-minded man. I see what I like and I might not live past next week, so I live for today."

"That's what I'm talking about, Divine. What happens when you get tired of me and find someone else? What can we expect for our future. I have a son and I want more children. Can you promise me a future? Because the drug game is limited. Can you promise me tomorrow?" Brooklyn was serious. She liked Divine, but her future meant more.

"Brooklyn, the only thing that I can promise you is my unconditional love and the willingness to strive for today so we could prepare for tomorrow."

"Divine, you just know the right things to say." She was smiling with tears of joy in her eyes.

"Nah, boo, I just let my heart be my guide. I want you to think about it," Divine said as he sipped his champagne.

"Boy, you're too much. I don't know why I let you get me open like this," Brooklyn said as she put her head under the water and took Divine's cock into her mouth.

Chapter 6

When Death Comes Knocking

Sheena, who lived across the hall, heard the commotion coming from Angel's apartment and called the police. Sheena was also abused by her abusive, alcoholic husband of seven years. Sheena had a four-year-old daughter named Melinda. Sheena and her daughter lived in the same battered women's shelter as Angel and Diamond. Sheena had moved into the building about two weeks before Angel. Sheena was a couple of years older than Angel. When Sheena heard all the commotion coming from Angel's apartment, the first thing she assumed was that Angel's abusive husband had found out where she and Diamond lived. This was a common fear of all the women who lived in the building. Women and their children were constantly moving out of the building because their abusers would find out their whereabouts and would harass them and sometimes even abuse them again. The tenants complained to the city about security in the building, but their complaints fell on deaf ears. Because of this, many of the women and children lived in fear.

Once Sheena called the police, she went to her door and looked out her peephole and noticed someone run out of the apartment. A few minutes later, she witnessed another person run out of the apartment. Both of them she recognized from off of the corner. Once she heard the front hallway door close behind them, she opened her door and walked across the hall to Angel's apartment whose door was wide open.

"Angel! Diamond!" Sheena called out as she walked into the apartment. Sheena noticed that the house reeked of feces and urine. "Oh, my God!" Sheena screamed as she covered her mouth with her hands from the sight.

Angel was lying in her own blood with her pants and panties pulled down to her ankles. Angel was bleeding from her head. She had a big gash in the back of her head. She was also bleeding from her ass and from in between her legs. Sheena automatically knew that Angel had been raped, even worse, she was sodomized. Sheena ran over to see if Angel was still breathing. Angel was alive, but barely. Sheena ran to her apartment and called 911 once again to let them know that an ambulance was needed. The 911 operator told Sheena that the police were pulling up to the building as they spoke and for her to show them where to go. Five minutes after the police had arrived, the ambulance arrived and rushed to Angel's apartment. They immediately started working on her, trying to revive her. Angel was slipping in and out of consciousness and was slowly going into shock. She had lost a lot of blood. The paramedics worked on her as they rushed her to the hospital. The police stayed and questioned Sheena about what she saw and heard. Sheena told the police that she didn't see anything. She said she heard the commotion and screaming and called 911. Sheena never told the police that she knew who did it. She would save that information for Diamond. The police asked Sheena who else stayed in the apartment with Angel. They also asked if Angel had a habit and if she was addicted to any drugs. They also asked Sheena did Angel owe any dealers any money, because they found crack at the scene. All of these questions were questions that Sheena knew nothing about. Angel kept her habit a secret. The police gathered all the information and then left. They told Sheena that Angel was in critical condition and it was touch and go for her. They told her that the paramedics were taking Angel to St. John's Hospital emergency room.

• • •

Diamond was hysterical. She called Brooklyn's house, but Brooklyn's aunt told her that Brooklyn was out with Divine. Diamond was a nervous wreck. She wished that her mother had paid the phone bill because she needed to speak with her urgently. She decided to call the lady next door, Mrs. Sheena.

Ring! Ring! Ring!

"Hello, Mrs. Sheena, this is Diamond. Can you go next door and get my mother for me?" Diamond said as she cried hysterically over the phone.

"Diamond, where are you? There's been an accident. Your mother..."

"Mrs. Sheena, what happened? Where's my mother? What happened to my mother?" Diamond said as she started to panic.

"Diamond, you need to get home now. Your mother needs you."

"Mrs. Sheena, what happened to my mother? Mrs. Sheena, please!!" Diamond's mouth was trembling and her hands were shaking.

"Someone broke into your house and assaulted Angel. She had to be rushed to the hospital," Sheena said not wanting to go into details about Angel being raped and sodomized or who she had seen running from the apartment.

Diamond hung up the phone and started to have an anxiety attack. She couldn't believe what Mrs. Sheena had just told her. All this was happening too fast. Angel was all she had. She had prayed that her mother was alright. Diamond was still shaken up about Ben's murder, now here she was stranded in N.C. and her mother was laid up in the hospital. Diamond felt so alone. She had tried to call Brooklyn, but was unsuccessful with reaching her. The next time she called, she told Brooklyn's aunt everything that had happened and told her to make sure that Brooklyn got in touch with her as soon as she got in.

Diamond was an emotional wreck. She feared losing Angel. So many crazy thoughts were running through her head about what could have happened. The obvious was her father, Rahmel, because they recently saw him. *He could have seen us when we were going downtown to get our hair and nails done and followed us.* Diamond thought to herself.

• • •

Divine and Brooklyn both rode in silence, both in deep thought about the pleasurable times they just had. Brooklyn was mesmerized by Divine. How she wished everything was for real. *Could he be just playing on my emotions? Is he sincere?* Brooklyn thought and wondered as she laid back in the plush leather seats listening to *Usher's* CD.

"What's up, boo? You aight? What's on your mind?" Divine asked Brooklyn as he steered the car with one hand and rubbed her thigh with the other.

She smiled. "I'm fine."

"Yes, I know you're fine, but I asked you how you were doing?" Divine replied. He focused back on the road.

"Actually, I'm doing a little too good and that scares me. I never had anything this easy, Divine. All my life I had it hard and then you come and offer me heaven. I wanna believe you, Divine. I do, but..." the tears came back out of nowhere.

"Hold up, boo, but is a contradiction. My word is my bond regardless to whom or what. To me, Brooklyn, the most important thing that a man has, well actually the three most important things are his mother, his wife and his word. And I lost my mother when I was nine years old. I'm not married, so the only thing I have left is my word. And I gave you my word that this is not a game. I want you to fulfill my second most important thing, to be my wife." Divine was dead serious and Brooklyn knew it.

Brooklyn sat back and contemplated what Divine had said to her. She was enjoying every bit of it, and was going to ride the cloud as far as it would take her.

When Divine pulled in front of Brooklyn's house, her little cousin ran out the door, up to the car and told Brooklyn that Diamond was in some trouble and had been calling like crazy. She told Brooklyn to call Diamond on her cell phone 911.

"Divine, let me use your phone," Brooklyn asked Divine. He passed the phone to her.

Divine turned his car off while Brooklyn dialed Diamond's number.

"Yo! Diamond, what's up?" Brooklyn asked concerned.

As soon as Diamond heard Brooklyn's voice, she started crying.

"Yo, Diamond, what's wrong? Diamond, calm down. What happened?" Brooklyn asked a little more firm than the first time.

"Brooklyn, somebody broke into our house and beat and robbed my mother and they rushed her to the hospital. Yo,

Brooklyn, that's not it. I'm stranded in N.C. Somebody robbed and murdered Big Ben," Diamond said as she stopped crying long enough to tell the story.

"Diamond, how is your mother?" Brooklyn inquired.

"I don't know. I'm stranded out here. I need you to go to St. John's Hospital. She's on the seventh floor. I've called Shymeek. He's on his way. He said he should be here in about six hours. So I'll just wait at the hotel until he gets here. I should be back in New York by one or two o'clock."

"Yo, Diamond, you be careful. I'ma have Divine drive me to the hospital right now."

"Brooklyn, as soon as you find anything out, make sure you call me, please?" Diamond begged.

As soon as Brooklyn hung up, she told Divine what had happened to Diamond in N.C. She also told him what had happened to Diamond's mother. Brooklyn asked Divine to drive her to the hospital to check on Angel. When Brooklyn told Divine of the story of Diamond transporting drugs to N.C. for a cat named Ben, aka Big Ben, it was too much of a coincidence to be true. *This couldn't be the same Big Ben. If it was, the world was too small.* Divine asked Brooklyn to describe Ben to him. And Brooklyn described the same Ben. He felt bad for Diamond, but he knew he was out of damn near fifty thousand. But in the drug game, there are always losses. You took the good with the bad. Divine had tried to warn Ben on how niggas got down in N.C. Them cats don't give a fuck if you have family down there. If you're from New York, to them you are a target.

As soon as they reached the hospital, Divine escorted Brooklyn to the front desk.

"Excuse me. The ambulance just brought in an Angel Weatherspoon," Brooklyn said to the nurse at the desk.

The nurse looked at her chart going down the list of entries.

"Yes, Mrs. Weatherspoon is being operated on by doctors as we speak. Y'all can have a seat and as soon as a doctor has the time or when they finish, someone'll be out here to speak to you," the chubby nurse said with an island accent.

"Thank you," Brooklyn said and she and Divine took a seat.

"Do you want something to drink?" Divine asked Brooklyn as he pointed at the vending machine.

"Yes, can you get me a Lipton iced tea? Thank you." Brooklyn made herself comfortable in the seat. She prepared herself for a long night.

As Divine walked off, the doctor came out of the back and spoke with Brooklyn. He told Brooklyn that Angel had been raped and sodomized and badly beaten. He told Brooklyn that Angel had lost a lot of blood and slipped into a coma once she went into shock. The doctor said that they did as much as they could for Angel and that only time would tell. As the doctor walked off, Brooklyn started crying. Angel was like a mother to her. Diamond and Brooklyn had been friends since the fifth grade, so she felt the effects of Angel and Diamond's pain. Divine walked back to Brooklyn with two bottles of iced tea. He sat down beside Brooklyn and placed his arms around her shoulders to comfort her. He knew how close she was with Diamond. He would put the word out for his people to put their ears to the streets to find out who was responsible.

"Brooklyn, it's going to be alright," Divine said as he passed her a wet paper towel.

"Divine, come on. I have to call Diamond back." Brooklyn and Divine walked out of the hospital.

Once in the car, Brooklyn called Diamond. When she told

Diamond that Angel was raped, Diamond dropped the phone and started screaming. Hearing Diamond screaming and crying broke Brooklyn's heart.

Once Brooklyn hung up the phone, she told Divine to drive to Diamond's apartment.

• • •

When Shymeek noticed Diamond's number followed by 911 on his pager, he called her right back. Diamond told him what was happening with her being stranded, but didn't get into details over the phone. She also explained to him that her mother was rushed to the hospital. Shymeek told Diamond to stay put, that he was on his way to get her. He calculated the hours it would take for him to reach her. As soon as he got off the phone, he left. Shymeek's first thought was, *What was she doing stranded in N.C.?* But that wasn't the issue right then. The issue was that his jewel was in trouble and he *never* second guessed his decision.

• • •

When Divine and Brooklyn pulled up in front of Diamond's building, the first thing Brooklyn noticed was that Pop and his crew, that stayed on the corner all types of nights, weren't there. The corner was empty. But Brooklyn just let the thought drift because everybody just knew that Rahmel was responsible. Brooklyn ran upstairs to Diamond's apartment and closed the apartment up. From what Brooklyn could see, nothing had been stolen. The house was turned upside down, but everything appeared to still be in place.

When Brooklyn exited the apartment, Mrs. Sheena opened her door and told Brooklyn to come to her apartment, that she had something to tell her.

"What's up, Sheena?" Brooklyn said, scurrying into the

neighbor's apartment.

"Do you know that dude Pop that is always on the corner with them crew of guys?" Mrs. Sheena asked in a whisper. "I seen him and another guy that's always on the corner run out of Angel's apartment," she added.

"I knew something was funny. All of a sudden, nobody is on the corner. I knew it," Brooklyn said. After saying good-bye, she stormed out of Sheena's apartment.

As soon as she got into Divine's car, Brooklyn told Divine everything that Sheena had told her and who she had seen running out of the crib. Immediately, Divine made a phone call.

Chapter 7

My Knight In Shining Armor

Brooklyn called Diamond back with the information she received from Sheena about Pop. Diamond swore that she would kill Pop as soon as she saw him, even though Brooklyn had told Diamond that Divine would handle Pop. The thought of that bitch ass nigga violating her mother was driving Diamond crazy. Diamond wanted to kill Pop so bad that her head started hurting. Shymeek wouldn't reach N.C. for another five to six hours and she was feeling exhausted and weak, not to mention her worrying about her mother and not being there with her. The fact that she was stranded in N.C., the fact that she had pissed on herself and could have been murdered only added to her headache. Her head felt as if someone was pounding on it with a sledgehammer. Diamond tried to relax herself. Before she knew it, she had dozed off into a deep sleep.

• • •

"Bitch, why the fuck are you always stressing a nigga? You don't need to worry about where I've been or who I have been with. All you need to worry about is me coming home to your sorry ass and this little spoiled bastard and me paying all the damn bills."

"Rahmel, if you're so unhappy and I'm so sorry, why don't you just leave? Let us be!"

"Bitch!" Rahmel screamed. His eyes were wide and his temper flared.

Smack!!! Rahmel cocked his hand back to take another swing.

As Angel hit the floor from the impact of Rahmel's hand, he stood over her and started punching and kicking Angel as she folded up into a fetal position to try and protect herself.

"Mommy! Mommy! Daddy, please, nooooo! Please Daddy, nooooo!" Diamond screamed.

Smack!!! "Little bitch, shut the fuck up."

Boom, boom, boom!!!

Diamond was awakened from her dream and the images that haunted her for years by somebody banging at the door. Since the day that Rahmel had battered her and Angel, she continually found herself haunted by the same images of Rahmel's abuse. Diamond had watched Rahmel physically abuse her mother like a rag doll before he turned on her.

Diamond looked at her watch. It was 7 a.m. the next morning. "Who is it?" Diamond asked. She was half asleep but still aware of her surroundings.

"Shymeek, Diamond. Open up."

Shymeek reached N.C. in 6-1/2 hours. He had stopped only once to fill up his tank. He had made it to N.C. but couldn't find the hotel and Diamond wasn't answering her cell phone. It took Shymeek over an hour to locate the hotel. As soon as Diamond opened the door, she jumped into Shymeek's arms. Shymeek was a sight for sore eyes. Diamond felt safe now. All she wanted to do now was get back to New York and see her mother.

• • •

Divine had called his man Meth and told him to go get Draz and Killa and for them to meet him at the store on Jefferson and Broadway. Divine had a coke spot that sold only 50 dollar bags of coke. The spot brought in about 25 to 30 thousand a week. Draz and Killa were two of Divine's lieutenants that grew up in the same project as he did. They were both about handling their business. Draz had just come home from doing a 5 to 15 year bid for attempted murder. Draz was a little older than Divine. Draz was good friends with Divine's older brother, Wonderful. Draz and Wonderful used to terrorize the hood. Their M.O. was S and M; Stick up and Murder. When Wonderful was murdered Draz and Divine became close. Divine and Draz had burnt down some spots owned by rival drug dealers from the islands who tried to open up shop on their block. These cats were opening crack houses all over Bedstuy and Brownsville in the early 90s. Divine was a young buck at the time. He couldn't have been any more than thirteen. After they ran the older Dreds off their block, Divine's name started ringing bells, not to mention he had a killer with him that moved out on command. Draz started using dope at a young age with Wonderful, and as he got older, his addiction got stronger and his thirst for blood was greater. Draz had recently found out that he had contracted the AIDS virus. Draz was fucking one of the baddest bitches in Brooklyn who had recently died from AIDS. So Draz had a death wish and he was Divine's walking gun. Since the day he found out about his sickness, he had become more vicious. This was how Draz made his living, and Divine was his only employer. So whenever Divine requested his presence, Draz knew it was a payday.

Killa was a youngin from the same project. The streets were all he had. His mother was strung out on crack and Killa had to fend for himself the best way he knew how. The streets

77

were his escape from his home reality. Killa had just turned seventeen and already had six bodies under his belt. Killa was up and coming in the murder game. His name had a little buzz in the streets. Killa loved the beef and glorified the drama. Killa had grown up wanting to be down with the street hustlers that were on the block. He idolized Draz and Divine. To him, they were real gangstas. And that's what he wanted to be. One day there was a big dice game on the corner of their block and Divine and Draz were there. One of the older cats at the game ass bet Killa and told him that he wasn't paying him shit and that his young ass better go home to his crackhead, dick sucking mother before something happened to his lil punk ass. Killa looked at Divine and Draz and their eyes said it all. Killa spent off. Fifteen minutes later, Killa returned to the dice game and pulled out an Uzi and laid the whole dice game down except Draz and Divine. Killa robbed the older cat that had disrespected him and let everybody else leave. As Killa started to walk off, the older cat told Killa that he was as good as dead. Killa spun around, squeezed the trigger killing the older cat and walked off. Killa got locked up, but nobody testified against him and they never had the murder weapon, so Killa beat the body. Divine told Draz to snatch Killa up and put him under the wing because he could be useful. From that day on, Killa was employed by Divine.

One day, Raul had a problem with another Columbian named Meguel in Miami. Meguel was married to Raul's sister. So Raul had called on Divine to handle the situation because he needed it taken care of by an outsider. Raul didn't want his brother-in-law's murder to come back on him. Meguel had fucked up some big money and Raul knew he couldn't let that go unanswered. This type of weakness was frowned upon in the cartel. So Meguel had to be dealt with and swiftly. At first,

Divine just wanted to send Draz and Killa but Raul asked for Divine to handle it personally. Divine knew it had to be handled with supreme caution, so Divine took Draz with him to Miami.

As soon as they reached Miami, Divine had a sit down with Raul. Raul explained the situation to Divine and that Meguel's murder could never come back on him. The hit had to look like a robbery or something. Raul gave Divine his sister's address with the stipulation that neither she nor the kids could witness their father being murdered nor could any harm come to his sister and children.

Divine and Draz staked out the house for two days straight. Each morning Draz dressed up like a bag lady going through the garbage collecting cans. He had a shopping cart filled with aluminum cans and other junk, while Divine stayed parked three houses down in a stolen SUV with tinted windows. Their break came on the third morning. Meguel exited his house and walked towards his car looking at a newspaper not paying any attention to Draz, who Meguel brushed off as a bum. Once Meguel reached his car, he fumbled with his car keys until he dropped them. As he bent down to pick up his keys, Draz went into his cart of cans and pulled out a 9mm with a silencer on it. Before Meguel could respond to the patting of feet running towards him, Draz was standing over him pointing his weapon at Meguel's head. Meguel froze for what seemed an eternity before Draz pulled the trigger.

Spit, pip, pip, pip!!! Miguel died from the first bullet's impact to the head. Draz checked his pockets and took everything he had of value. He snatched the car keys off the ground, jumped into Meguel's car and pulled off. Divine started up his car and followed behind Draz. They dumped Meguel's car and set it ablaze, then got into the stolen SUV and drove back into the city.

The Miami's paper read, "Carjack, robbery turns bloody." The newspaper said that a witness that was taking out the garbage saw a bum crackhead looking lady digging in the garbage looking for aluminum cans for the five cent deposits when she noticed the victim come out of his house walking to his luxury car. The witness told the reporters that the bum must have seen dollar signs when she saw the car that the victim was driving.

The finger was never pointed at Raul. Raul tried to give Divine fifty thousand for his deed but Divine refused it and told Raul that it was done as a favor. Divine gave Draz 10 g's out of his own pocket.

Once Meth walked into the spot with Draz and Killa, Divine told Meth that he needed him to put in twelve hours at the spot because the regular worker had to go to court. Meth was Divine's all-purpose runner. He used Meth for whatever he needed done. Meth wasn't no gangsta nor was he a killer, so Divine never involved him with the gun play. Divine, Draz and Killa all walked to the room in the back of the store. Divine explained to them what had taken place with Brooklyn's friend's mother and about the nigga Pop and his little crew. Divine explained to them that Pop was a small time local nickel and dime crack selling ass nigga that never left the block. So it shouldn't be hard to find the cat because the corner was all he knew. Divine gave them both 5 g's a piece and told them that he wanted this Pop cat dealt with and quick. Draz and Killa took the money and left. They had a job to do. This Pop cat would soon be dead. They left the spot headed for Bergen and Franklin to catch a thief; a faggot mutha fucka who had to *take* pussy. They were gonna love killing the bitch ass nigga.

When Divine was about to leave the spot, he gave Meth a

couple of bags of weed and told him that lil Mike would be there to relieve him when his twelve hours were up and that Kyzim would stop by to check on him later. Kyzim was one of Divine's lieutenants. Divine left the spot and called Brooklyn.

• • •

"Yo, son, the police just left from that bitch Angel's crib. Why you had to rape that bitch, son?" Regg and Pop were in the living room of Pop's crib.

"Man, fuck that crackhead bitch, son. I've been fucking that bitch for a while. Now that she get a lil money, the bitch wanna act funny," Pop said taking a drag from his PCP laced cigarette.

"Yo, dog, what if she dies?" The dust had Regg alive and aware. He was scared to death of what went down at Angel's crib.

"Then we wouldn't have to worry about her telling on us. Dead people tell no tales," Pop said as he smoked his last bag of wet. "Besides, that bitch ain't gonna say anything because she don't want her daughter to find out that she was smoking. Ya heard?" Pop smiled.

"What about the police?"

Pop's smile immediately left his face. "Man, would you stop worrying. That bitch ain't gonna say nothing. She's a crackhead that has too much to hide." Pop took another drag then went to pass the joint to Regg.

"I hope so, son," Regg said as he reached for the blunt that Pop had.

"Yo, son, we're aight. Nobody seen us go in the building or come out. All we have to do is stay low for a couple of days until the heat dies down. I'll get crackhead D-Brown to run us the heads to my crib, so we don't have to miss any of this money," Pop said as he got up to go across the hall to get D-Brown.

• • •

During the ride back to New York, Diamond told Shymeek what she was doing in N.C. and how Ben was murdered the night before making a sale. Diamond also told Shymeek everything about her and her mother being abused by her father and how they had it hard while he drove around in all types of luxury cars and she and her mother struggled just to make it from day to day. She told Shymeek it was the reason she transported drugs out of town for Ben. Because she would never strip or sell her pussy because she had too much respect for herself. Diamond didn't tell Shymeek that Ben was paying her for sex once a week or whenever he came back to Brooklyn. She would keep that part to herself. Shymeek was touched by Diamond's strength and will to endure the drama that she had been through. He felt bad for her. He wanted to be the one that made the difference in her life. When Diamond told Shymeek what had happened to her mother, Shymeek couldn't believe it. He had just met Angel the other day. *Who could violate such a beautiful person?* Shymeek thought to himself as he drove. Diamond started crying every time she thought about Pop raping and sodomizing her mother. Diamond reclined her seat and let her mind travel. She was glad that Shymeek was with her.

"Shymeek, are you my knight in shining armor here to take me away from all of this hell?" Diamond didn't look at Shymeek when she asked him this. She was afraid of what he might say.

When Diamond and Brooklyn were younger, they always said that one day their prince charming was going to come and sweep them off their feet. But instead of riding on a horse, he was going to be driving a Benz.

Shymeek took a second to look at Diamond before he refocused on the road. "Only if you allow me to, Diamond. You deserve much more than the hand that life dealt you. And if you allow me, we can change that. I'm willing to help you make that change."

Diamond now looked at him. "Shymeek, it's hard to believe the things I've been through in my short lived life, and I'm still standing. All I want to do is finish school, but it's hard when you have to struggle just to make it through the week," Diamond said as she dried her eyes with a damp washrag she took from the hotel room.

"Don't worry, Diamond, I'm going to take care of you. I want it to be about you and me. I promise I'll take care of you and make sure you finish school. You'll have whatever you need and whatever it takes, we'll do it together. As soon as we come from the hospital from seeing your mother, I want you to pack all of your things from that apartment and I'm moving you and your mother in with me. I have a house in Brownsville. I want you to stay with me. I hardly use the house because I'm on the road a lot."

"Shymeek, you would do that for me?" Diamond asked as she looked at Shymeek in disbelief.

"Listen, Diamond, if you gonna be my girl, the sky's the limit. We can all live comfortably in my house. Y'all would love it." He smiled.

Diamond just laid her head back and contemplated everything that Shymeek had said. She was feeling him. Diamond couldn't wait to make love to him. She would do her best to rock his world. Diamond dozed off to sleep thinking about making love to Shymeek to try and clear her mind of what she would see when she reached the hospital.

As soon as they reached Brooklyn, Shymeek drove directly to the hospital. Shymeek woke Diamond up when they were pulling into St. John's Hospital parking lot. The rest that Diamond got on the trip back to New York did her a lot of good. The events over the last couple of hours in her life had exhausted her. Her body had shut down. Everything came crashing down on her at once when she entered the hospital room and saw her mother laid up with all types of machines hooked up to her and tubes coming out of her mouth and nose. Angel looked so battered and frail. Her face was swollen and bruised and her eyes were swollen shut. Diamond took one look at her mother and lost it. She started screaming and crying. Shymeek did his best to prevent Diamond from hurting herself. The doctors rushed in to help Shymeek calm Diamond down. The reality of Angel's condition really hit Diamond when she saw her mother lying in the hospital's bed helpless and unresponsive. The sight of Diamond's reaction to seeing her mother crushed Shymeek. He wanted to hurt whoever was responsible for this savage act. But for now, his main focus was to make sure that Diamond was alright. Shymeek picked Diamond up and carried her out of the hospital, put her into his truck and drove her to his house. Once Shymeek reached the crib, he laid Diamond in his bed and made her some hot cocoa.

"Diamond, I want you to try to get some rest and relax. I'ma go to y'all's apartment and pack as much stuff as I can for you. Is there anything specific you want me to bring you?"

Diamond told Shymeek where she had her money stashed then gave him the keys to the apartment. Shymeek kissed Diamond on the forehead and told her to try and get some rest and that he would be back shortly. As Shymeek left the crib, Diamond closed her eyes and more tears fell while she thought of the images of her mother in her condition.

• • •

Draz and Killa circled the block numerous times until they spotted a fiend. They pulled up to the fiend and called him to the car.

"Yo, what's up? Who got it?" Draz asked.

"What's up? What 'cha want?" the fiend anxiously replied.

"We looking for Pop. We copped from him yesterday. We want some crills."

"How much?" The crackhead was looking to come up. He was thirsty.

"Do you work for P? Because we only want his shit. We have fifty dollars." Draz showed the fiend two twenties and a ten dollar bill.

"Yeah, I'm running for him because he's not seeing anybody today. So give me the money. I'll go and get it for you," D-Brown said.

"So you can run off with our money, hell, nah. I never dealt with you before. Tell Pop it's B," Draz said making up the first name that came to his head.

"Man, it's not that type of party. It's just that Pop is on the low right now and he's not dealing with nobody today. That's why he got me out here," D-Brown said as he accepted the money from Killa.

"Yo, if you come correct, we'll take care of you, aight? A yo, I hope this is Pop's shit. If it's not, we're bringing it back," Draz retorted.

"Yeah, it's Pop's shit, don't worry about it," D-Brown said as he ran into the building.

Draz and Killa watched as D-Brown ran into the building.

They looked to see where he had run to. They noticed that he didn't go up any stairs. That meant that Pop lived on the first floor. They were gonna cop from D-Brown all day to get Pop's confidence and then request to cop from Pop themselves because they had been copping from him all day and they wanted a play.

Each time they came, they copped at least fifty dollars worth of work. And each time D-Brown would tap the work. He was loving Draz and Killa.

As they waited in the car for D-Brown to return, they noticed a white Range Rover pull up in front of the building on the corner.

"Yo, Draz, ain't that the music producer cat that do beats for Roc-A-Fella?" Killa asked as he pointed to Shymeek who had run into Diamond's building.

"Yeah, that's that nigga, son. I wish we wasn't on detail because I know that nigga is holding. Ya heard? That rap money is long."

"Word. I know that's right!" Killa said as he noticed D-Brown coming out of the building.

D-Brown ran up to the car and handed them some skimpy shit.

"Damn, nigga, this is fifty dollars worth?" Draz asked observing the product.

"Yeah, don't worry about it. This was the last of the bag. Pop said he'll take care of you when you come back," D-Brown said lying through his dirty teeth. "And this shit is the bomb so the size don't really matter," D-Brown said as he started running to another fiend he had waiting for him.

As Draz pulled off, Killa called Divine and let him know that that situation would soon be taken care of.

Each time they came back to cop from Pop, they took the

work to Meth and told him to give the shit they copped from Pop to all the regulars. On their last trip, they noticed Shymeek leaving the building with a suitcase.

"Yo, D-Brown," Draz holla'd from the hooptie they were in.

D-Brown noticed the car and immediately ran over to the car.

"Okay, the big spenders are back. What's up?" D-Brown said as he stuck his head into the car's window.

"Yeah, that's exactly what we're talking about. Big spenders all day. It's time for us to get a play. We've been coming all day and Pop hasn't looked out for us yet."

"Don't worry, dog, I'ma tell him. What y'all need?"

"We have a yard but we wanna see Pop ourselves. Don't worry if he looks out for us, we got you, aight."

"Hold up. I'll be right back. Let me see if Pop wanna deal with you."

"Man, you know we have been spending with you all day. And we bought from him yesterday, he knows us."

"Aight, hold up, I'll be right back," D-Brown said and ran into the building.

"Yo, son, are you ready?" Draz said as he checked his gun.

"Yeah, son, you know I'm always ready for that 187 on a fraud ass nigga."

"Yo, Killa, if the nigga don't want to deal with us, we're just gonna make this crackhead ass nigga show us where the nigga live. Ya heard?" Draz said as he noticed D-Brown in Pop's building doorway waving for them to come in.

"Yo, son, it's on."

Chapter 8
I Have A Surprise For You

As soon as Divine hung up from Draz, Brooklyn called him. Divine told Brooklyn that as soon as he got through with what he was doing he would swing by and pick her up. "Yo, wear something sexy for me, aight. I'll see you in a few," Divine said as he hung up the phone. Divine's pager went off again. When Divine checked it, he had two pages. He never heard the first page. They must have paged him at the same time. One was from his man Mo'Better and the other one was from an older cat that he sold weight to who hustled on the other side of Brooklyn.

Divine called them both back and told them to meet him at the building on Hancock.

Divine and Mo'Better both arrived in front of the building at the same time. Divine got out of his car and motioned for Mo'Better to follow him. As Divine entered the building, lil Remo and Black were on security detail. They both peaced Divine in unison and gave Mo'Better a killer look. They both had their guns displayed. Divine whispered something in lil Remo's ear and Remo pulled out his cell phone and made a call. Divine and Mo'Better went upstairs to the second floor. As they entered the apartment, Mo'Better placed the Louis Vuitton bag on the table that contained his money plus the money he owed Divine for the five keys.

"Yo, son, everything is there. The 45.5 I owe plus 95 for the same thing," Mo'Better said as he sat back in the chair while Divine counted the money.

"Damn, Mo', you're doing pretty damn good for yourself, son," Divine said to Mo' as he passed Mo'Better a complementary bottle of Crystal that he gave all of his people that bought 10 or more of them things.

"Man, look who's talking, mister give all of his big spenders a complementary bottle of Crystal. Now that's what I call big pimping. All you're missing is that one special lady at your side or two. If you know like I know," Mo'Better said as he cracked the bottle of Crystal and took it to the head.

"Yo, Mo', believe it or not, that's in the works."

"I hope so, son, it's time for you to make some seeds to spend all this damn money on."

"Man, just because you have kids all over Brooklyn and Harlem, don't mean that I have to follow in your footsteps," Divine said as he and Mo'Better both started laughing.

As Divine finished counting the money, lil Remo entered the apartment with a suitcase. He placed the suitcase on the coffee table. Then he whispered in Divine's ear that somebody was waiting downstairs in their car to come upstairs.

"Yo, is it Rahmel?" Divine asked Remo.

"Yeah. He said that he called and spoke to you already."

"Yeah, he did. Go tell him to give me fifteen minutes and then come up. Aight?"

Lil Remo left out the door and Divine pulled out the tester for Mo'Better to check the coke.

"Yo, son, you know that's not for us. We've been doing this

together too long. Your word is gold to me, son. Is this that same raw shit you gave me the last time?" he asked.

"Man, you can step on that shit six times and it'll still be the best coke in New York. Ya feel me?"

Mo'Better closed the suitcase, gave Divine a pound and proceeded out the door. At the same time, Rahmel was coming into the apartment.

"What's up, Mo? How can a nigga like me get some of that Harlem money?" Rahmel said to Mo' as he exited the apartment.

"What's up, Rah? It seems like every time I'm here, you're here. That means you're doing something right. You don't need Harlem, Brooklyn got you eating well I see," Mo'Better said as he walked out the door and down the stairs.

"What's up, Rahmel?"

"What's up, Vine. You know what time it is. I need two of them things."

"Ole school, I got 'cha. When you gonna step your game up and cop ten of these things? I have some good prices for you."

"Don't worry, young blood, as soon as I'm ready, I'ma see you. Ya heard?"

Divine told lil Remo to bring up two keys. When lil Remo left, Divine rolled up a blunt, kicked it to Rahmel while they waited for lil Remo to bring Rahmel the work. As soon as lil Remo returned, Divine gave Rahmel the two keys and Rahmel counted out 24 g's and passed it to Divine. Rahmel put the two keys in his knapsack and left the apartment. Divine really didn't trust Rahmel. There was something about him. Divine felt a certain vibe from him. Rahmel had a lot of shiesty ways about him. When Rahmel left, Divine called Brooklyn and told her he was on his way.

• • •

As Shymeek put the last of Diamond's stuff into his truck, he noticed two dudes sitting in a hooptie staring at him. Shymeek wondered if the dudes had anything to do with Diamond's mother being raped. The cat behind the wheel looked sick in the face, like he had that monster. His face was pale with dark spots. You could always tell somebody that had that shit. He had murderous eyes that sunk into his eye sockets. *I pray that this cat didn't have anything to do with Angel's rape,* Shymeek thought to himself as he jumped into his truck and watched the two cats get out of their car and go into the building with a third cat who looked like he was on a mission. Shymeek started his truck up and pulled off.

On his way back to the house, Shymeek stopped at the Jamaican restaurant and ordered jerk chicken dinners with two carrot juices for both him and Diamond. Jamaican food was Shymeek's favorite food. Shymeek paid for the dinners and as he was leaving out the door, he received a page. As Shymeek got into his truck, he looked at his two-way and smiled. He had one more stop to make before he went home to Diamond.

• • •

Draz and Killa jumped out of the car and followed D-Brown to an apartment at the end of the hallway in the back. D-Brown knocked on the door and Pop told him that the door was open and to come in. Draz and Killa followed behind D-Brown as he led them into the living room where Pop and Regg were playing video games on the big screen TV and smoking wet.

"Yo, Pop, what's up?" Draz asked waiting to see which one would respond to make sure they had the right person.

"What's up? What y'all want?" Pop asked never once taking his eyes off of the TV as he continued to play the game.

As soon as Pop responded, Draz and Killa pulled out their guns. At the same time, Killa kicked D-Brown to the floor. Regg jumped up out of reflex and Killa laid him down immediately.

BUNK, BUNK, BUNK, BUNK!!!

Regg's body collapsed to the floor as blood gushed from his head wounds. D-Brown started screaming. Killa walked up to D-Brown, stood over him and aimed at his head.

BUNK, BUNK!!

D-Brown's body started convulsing as his life force left his body and his blood oozed out of his head, nose and mouth. Pop froze as he looked into Draz's eyes with a pleading stare.

"Yo, son, you raped a woman that had some pretty powerful friends. You got to answer for what you did," Draz said as he pointed his gun at Pop's face.

"Yo, son, I don't know what you're talking about. I had nothing to do with raping nobody. If it's the drugs you want, I have an ounce on the table," Pop said as he slowly inched for his 357 he had under the pillow next to him.

Draz peeped his movement and allowed him to get his hand under the pillow to let him think that he could pull it off. Pop knew his chances were slim to none, but he had nothing to lose. He knew he was gonna die anyway. So he decided to make his move. As soon as Pop moved his body an inch, Draz squeezed the trigger.

POP, POP, POP, POP!!!

Pop's body slumped over on the couch and Draz turned to Killa and said to him, "Let's go." Before they left the house, Killa ran into the kitchen and snatched the ounce of crack off of the table. They left the apartment and jumped into their hooptie and pulled off. While Draz drove, Killa called Divine to let him know that Pop was history.

• • •

Divine pulled up in front of Brooklyn's house and beeped his horn. Brooklyn ran to the window and told Divine that she would be right out. Brooklyn stepped out the front door looking breathtaking dressed in a strapless Dolce & Gabbana evening gown. The dress hugged Brooklyn's every curve. Divine grabbed his manhood and started caressing himself subconsciously. *Damn! I got me a winner. Shorty is all that,* Divine thought to himself. Brooklyn got into the car and gave Divine a kiss, revealing all of her assets as she bent over and stuck her tongue in Divine's mouth.

"What's up, Boo? You're looking real tasty. Is all that for me?" Divine asked as he pulled off.

"How was your day, Daddy?" Brooklyn asked as she blushed from Divine's comment.

"My day just got a little brighter now that I'm in your presence," he beamed.

"Oh boy, hush. You swear you're a playa," Brooklyn said as she punched him on the arm in a playful manner.

"Girl, you just don't know, do you?" He glanced at her.

"Know what? Divine, don't start talking in riddles."

"How serious I am about you and me."

"I hope so but time will tell it all. Where are we going anyway that you wanted me to get all sexy?" She rolled her eyes seductively.

"Girl, I just wanted you to get sexy for me! I have to be taking you somewhere for you to get sexy for a nigga? Nah, but it's a surprise, just relax. Brooklyn, do me a favor and go into the glove compartment and get that blunt and roll up this purple haze for us, to put us where we want to be. To put us in the right frame of mind." Divine glanced at her again with a smile.

"There you go again, to put us in the right frame of mind for what?" Brooklyn gave her man that sexy look again.

"Girl, you sure ask a lot of questions. Don't worry, you can trust me." Divine placed his attention back on the road and enjoyed his natural high.

Thirty minutes later, Divine was pulling up in front of the Apollo Theatre. They both were high as a kite feeling the effects of the purple haze.

"Daddy, what's going on in the Apollo tonight?" Brooklyn was looking at the long line of people standing outside the famous establishment.

"Amateur night, boo."

As Divine and Brooklyn exited the car, Brooklyn could feel all eyes on them. It seemed as if everybody knew Divine. From the car to the entrance, Divine was stopped five times as people gave him pounds and hugs. Divine and Brooklyn didn't have to wait in line like everyone else; they walked right in.

"Nigga, you think you're a star, don't you?" Brooklyn said to Divine as he led her into the theater as they laughed.

Once they were seated, Divine's two-way went off again. It had been vibing since they left Brooklyn's house. Divine checked his pager and recognized Draz's code. Draz and Killa always put 187 behind whatever number they were calling from. Divine knew he had to take this call.

"Boo, I'll be right back. I'ma go to the bathroom and take this call. Do you need anything from the stand?"

"Nah, Daddy, I'm alright. I just want you to hurry up back and don't get lost on me," she said smiling.

As Divine entered the hallway, he called Draz back.

"Draz, what's up, son?"

"Yo, Vine, you know what's up. That situation is history. Ya heard?"

"Aight, son. I'll hit you back when I get back around the way. Peace!"

Divine hung the cell phone up and was headed back into the theater when somebody called his name.

"Yo, Divine, Divine."

Divine turned around and noticed a chick named China that he was fucking coming towards him. They called her China because she was a mix between black and Hawaiian and she looked Chinese.

"Oh, what's up, China?" Divine extended his hand.

"You're what's up. Why haven't you called me? You just hit the pussy and forget about the bitch, huh?"

China was from Queens. She ran with a wild pack of chicks that be setting niggas up. Divine had used her and her crew a couple of times. China was a dime and the sex was the bomb, but she was a little too wild to make her wifey.

"Nah, it's not like that. I've just been a little busy lately. Who are you here with?"

"Divine, you know I roll with my crew. Why? You want me to slide off with you, so you can give me some of that dick?" she asked, trying to reach for his crotch.

"Nah, it's not like that. I'm here with my lil shorty."

"Oh word. That's why you haven't called a sista, huh?" China put her hands on her hips.

"China, you know how you and I gets down. Shorty or not, you know I'ma holla at you. As a matter of fact, I'ma get at you in a couple of days. I got something for you to do for me. Aight?"

"Divine, you know I'm with that as long as some paper *and* dick is involved. Ya heard?"

"China, I got you. I'ma call you in a couple of days, so be ready."

"I wish you hurry up and stop frontin'. I'm trying to get some more of that," China said as she rubbed up against his crotch and walked back into the auditorium.

Divine's dick stood to attention. He knew he could have taken China right into the bathroom and fucked the shit out of her because she was down for anything he said. But Divine wasn't trying to fuck up what he was trying to build with Brooklyn. He'd call China in a few days and use her for some work. A couple of Panamanians had recently moved on the block and opened up a store at the corner. The word was that they were trying to set up shop and Divine wasn't to have that. So he would send China in to feel them out and to come back and let him know what was going on. But of course he would fuck her first. Divine always credited his success to his ability to stay one step ahead of his competition. He had put too much work in to let some foreigners eat off of his blood, sweat and tears. They would be dealt with immediately.

As Divine walked back into the auditorium, he recognized China and her crew to the left and of course, they were the loudest group of people in the auditorium. Divine and Brooklyn were seated in the front close to the stage. As he walked to where they were seated, he noticed how marvelous Brooklyn looked as she laughed at the comedian that was hosting the show. Brooklyn was the finest thing in there. When Divine took his seat, he kissed Brooklyn on her cheek.

"Did you miss me?" he asked.

"Of course. Did you get lost or something?" Brooklyn asked as she licked and nibbled on Divine's ear.

"I had to make an important phone call. Oh yeah, that situation with that Pop cat is taken care of," Divine said to

Brooklyn as he gave her that look.

Chapter 9

A Gift Of Life

Shymeek entered the crib at two in the morning. He figured that Diamond would be angry. He had left her to go pick up her clothes from her mother's apartment after they left the hospital from visiting Diamond's mother. That was around 5 p.m. Shymeek peeped into the bedroom and Diamond was fast asleep. Shymeek decided to take a shower to wash off whatever scent he might have had on him that would let Diamond know that he was just with another woman. If Diamond asked him where he had gone and what took him so long, he would tell her that he had to go to the studio and do an emergency track for a remix of one of his artist's singles. After Shymeek washed up, he dried himself off, put on his Fendi bathrobe and went into the kitchen to heat up the Jamaican food he bought earlier. When Shymeek walked into the bedroom, Diamond was lying across the bed on top of the covers in just her bra and thong. *Damn! She look good enough to eat, laying there like an angel*, Shymeek thought to himself as the guilt of the unnatural sex he had indulged in for the last couple of hours came to his thoughts. *"Damn, if anybody ever finds out about my secret life, I'm through,"* Shymeek said to himself as he placed the food on the night table. Shymeek bent over and kissed Diamond on the forehead.

"Diamond. Diamond," Shymeek said as he gently shook Diamond to awaken her.

Diamond opened her eyes and looked at Shymeek as if she didn't recognize him. She tried to focus her eyesight.

"Hey, where have you been? You've been gone all day," Diamond said as she looked at her Jacob watch to see what time it was.

"I had to go to the studio and do a remix for one of my artists who had a deadline to meet. I stopped at the Jamaican spot and bought us some food. Are you hungry? I also put all the stuff you asked me to get out of the apartment for you in the living room," Shymeek replied, quickly switching the subject of where he was.

"Shymeek, did you bring me my toothbrush, shampoo and all my other cosmetics?"

"No, but I did stop by the pharmacy and buy you all new shit. It's all laid out on the bathroom sink for you."

"Shymeek, you're the best," Diamond said as she got up and walked into the bathroom to deal with some refinement.

Shymeek's dick got hard as he watched Diamond strut her 34-26-36 frame across the room into the bathroom. Shymeek had yet to hit the pussy, but he knew Diamond had some good pussy, especially if he hit it from the back with that tight firm ass of hers. Shymeek couldn't wait to get in between them thighs. But he wasn't gonna press it tonight. Besides, having just finished freaking, he was kinda tired. Shymeek didn't figure her to want to fuck him tonight after all she had been through anyway, but if she gave him any kind of inclination that she was with fucking, he would tear that pussy up. Maybe that's what she needed, maybe some hard dick would clear her mind of all her problems. Shymeek was attracted to Diamond in a big way. She was what he liked in a woman; 5' 3, 125 pounds with bowed legs. Diamond had a golden brown complexion and straight black hair. Although she was young, she had what he was looking for. Shymeek was torn between his secret life and wanting to make Diamond his girl. But his secret would have to forever remain a secret. Whatever else he needed to satisfy his sexual desires, he knew how to get them taken care of. Diamond came out of the bathroom and walked towards Shymeek with a provocative smile on her face.

"Shymeek, there's something that I've been wanting to give you since the first time I met you," Diamond said as she walked up to him and pulled him up off the bed, untied is robe and stuck her hand down his boxers.

When Diamond started to stroke Shymeek's manhood, he moaned from her touch.

"Do you want me, Shymeek?" Diamond asked as she stroked his cock harder and faster. She felt him beginning to rise for the occasion.

"Oh, yes, Diamond, more than you can imagine." Shymeek gasped, then swallowed hard.

Diamond pulled Shymeek's robe off and his boxers down. As Shymeek stepped out of his boxers, Diamond pushed him back onto the bed, bent down in front of him and proceeded to give him some head. Diamond started licking the head of his cock and then she started sucking and licking on his balls as he moaned in ecstasy. Diamond sucked the head of his manhood as if it was a Charms blow pop. At the same time that Diamond sucked on the head of his cock, she stroked his shaft harder and faster. Diamond relaxed her throat and took all of Shymeek's manhood into her mouth until his testicles were slapping against her chin with every thrust of Shymeek's hips.

"Oh, yes! Yes! Diamond, yeah, right there!" Shymeek moaned as he rubbed his hands through Diamond's hair.

Diamond pulled Shymeek out of her mouth, looked into his eyes and asked him was he serious or did he just want some pussy? Shymeek pulled Diamond up off her knees and close to his face. He whispered to her that he was willing to give her the world.

"In that case, come on, I have a world to give you," Diamond said as she laid on her stomach, supported her weight with her forearms and raised her ass to the air. "It's yours, Daddy."

Shymeek entered Diamond from the back. Her insides felt so hot and warm, not to mention tight. Shymeek wanted to cry. With every stroke, Diamond met Shymeek with her own thrust of her ass as she moved her hips in a circular motion making sure Shymeek's manhood didn't leave any parts of her womanhood untouched. The harder and faster Shymeek thrust and banged Diamond from the back, the more she screamed for him to fuck her harder and faster. This continued all night until they both collapsed in each other's arms.

• • •

"Yo, Alfonso, that nigga shit is kinda tight. When you enter the building, he has two cats that's armed at all times standing in the hallway. Not to mention that everybody outside is hustling for him."

"Rahmel, you said that he took you upstairs to a second floor apartment. Do you know if he has any more apartments in the building?"

"I don't know, but one of his runners brings him the drugs from some place other than the apartment. He leaves and then comes back with the work. It's possible that he has another crib where he keeps the weight at. I doubt that they keep that shit far away. Divine sells that shit like it's candy. Most of the people he deals with buys at least ten or better."

"Rahmel, why do you come to us with this? What's in it for you?" Alfonso asked.

"Alfonso, like I told you before, I know that you and your people are about your business and I see opportunity. I know how you Panamanians get down. Y'all knew these young brothers were getting plenty of paper off of this block, that's why y'all opened up a store on their block. What I want? I want the building. It's a gold mine. With y'all backing me, we can get rich," Rahmel said convincingly.

"It sounds good, but what makes you think that we need you to help us get rich?"

"I didn't say to make *you* rich, I said that *we* could get rich. Y'all know that the money on this block is booming, but Divine and his lil crew of crack dealers is in y'alls way. Furthermore, I know the neighborhood. I've lived in Brooklyn over forty years. Y'all *will* need me."

"Listen, this is what we're going to do. This Divine cat we're going to leave to you. If you handle him, we'll provide you with all the work you need. You can have the block and the building. You just have to cop the weight from us. Agreed?" said Alfonso.

"I can agree to your terms, but I need the manpower and the guns to move on Divine."

"Don't worry, we'll provide you with whatever you need as long as you take care of your part of the deal." Alfonso leaned back in his chair and clasped his hands together.

"Aight then, it's good as done," Rahmel said as he got up, shook Alfonso's hand and left the store.

When Rahmel left the store, Divine's building was busy

with its normal activity; making money. *All of this will soon be mine,* Rahmel thought to himself as he jumped into his Lexus and pulled off.

• • •

"Yo, lil Remo, isn't that that nigga Rahmel coming out of the Panamanian's store right there?" Meth asked.

"Yeah, that's that cat," Remo answered.

"I'ma page Divine and let him know that this nigga is over here fucking with these cats," Meth said as he pulled out his cell phone.

• • •

When Divine and Brooklyn left the Apollo, Divine drove to New Jersey.

"Divine, where are we going?" Brooklyn asked.

"There you go again with all the fifty questions. Just relax and enjoy the ride. I have something to show you," Divine said as he turned on the car's DVD player. "Just lay back and enjoy the movie. We'll be there in a minute."

Thirty minutes later, Divine was pulling up to a big ass house in New Jersey. The house was twice the size of the house he had in Queens. Brooklyn wondered who lived in the house. Whoever it belonged to was holding. Brooklyn couldn't hold it any longer. She wanted to know whose house they were going to.

"Divine, who lives here?" she asked excitedly.

"This is what I wanted to show you. This is my house. You are the only one who knows about this house. Come on, I have some more to show you." Divine jumped out of the car and pulled Brooklyn through the driver's side door with him.

As soon as Divine opened the door, a little girl came running from the back with a heavy-set lady behind her. The little girl jumped into Divine's arms.

"Daddy, Daddy, Daddy," the little girl screamed in joy as Divine took her into his arms.

Brooklyn's mouth dropped to the floor from what she just heard and witnessed. This little girl was a female version of Divine. *Why he never told me about his daughter?* Brooklyn thought to herself.

"Girl, what are you still doing up at this time of night?" Divine asked as he kissed his daughter on the forehead. "Brooklyn, this is my precious jewel Heaven. Say peace, Heaven."

"Peace. What's your name?" Heaven asked Brooklyn in the cutest voice.

"Hey, beautiful, my name is Brooklyn," Brooklyn said as she squeezed Heaven's cheeks. "Divine, she's a doll. Why didn't you tell me about this angel before?"

"Brooklyn! That's where me and my mommy used to live," Heaven said as she got down out of Divine's arms.

"Yeah, I live in Brooklyn too," Brooklyn said, responding to the little princess' remark.

"So, why did you say that your name is Brooklyn?" Heaven was looking up at Brooklyn so Brooklyn knelt down allowing Heaven to get a closer look at her while they spoke.

"Because that's what everybody calls me."

"Oh, okay," Heaven said and ran back to the back.

"And this lady right here is my mother/baby sitter/housekeeper/everything. But you can call her Mrs. Hardy." Divine smiled when he introduced Brooklyn to his mother.

"Nice to meet you, Mrs. Hardy," Brooklyn said. She shook Divine's mother's hand.

"Nice to meet you as well, Brooklyn. That's what you said your name was, right?"

"My name is Maria, but all my friends call me Brooklyn."

"Okay, then Brooklyn is good enough for me. If you all are hungry, there's some food on the stove, you just have to heat it up," Mrs. Hardy said. Then she followed behind Heaven.

"Ma," Divine called out to his mother before she exited the living room. "What's Heaven still doing up at this time of night?"

"Boy, you know that girl has problems going to bed when you're not home. She's afraid that you're going to leave her again," Mrs. Hardy said as she walked out the living room door.

"Divine, you are full of surprises. Divine, where is Heaven's mother, if you don't mind me asking?"

"Her mother died from cancer right before I got locked up. That's what my mother meant when she said that my daughter was afraid that I would leave her again. She had lost both her parents in the same year. That was a lot for a three-year-old. She's seven now and she's my world. I want you to be a part of that world, Brooklyn," he said sincerely.

Brooklyn gazed into Divine's killer's eyes and saw a gentle soul. Right then she realized that she wanted to spend the rest of her life with this man.

"Brooklyn, come on, I have something else to show you." Divine pulled Brooklyn by her arm and led her up some spiral stairs that led to the second floor of the house into his bedroom.

Over Divine's bed he had a painted portrait of himself, Heaven and Heaven's mother. Heaven was the spitting image of her mother. She was beautiful.

"Divine, what was her name?" Brooklyn stared at the portrait.

"Her name was Fatimah."

"Did she believe in what you believe in?" She looked at him.

"What, was she a five percenter? Yes, she was." He looked at Brooklyn when he spoke but returned his gaze at the picture. He then looked over at another portrait. Divine walked to the other picture that was hanging on the wall. It was Divine with two other people in the picture. The biggest one out of the group looked like he could have been Divine's brother.

"Divine, who are the two people in the picture with you?" Brooklyn pointed.

"The big dude is my brother, Wonderful. He was murdered. The other dude is his man Draz. They terrorized Brooklyn back in the days. Draz, he still runs with me."

Divine went behind the picture and there was a safe behind it. He opened the safe and there were stacks of money neatly piled in six rolls. There was also a black box and papers.

"Can you guess how much money is in this safe?" Divine asked Brooklyn as he pulled out the black box from the safe.

"How much? About a hundred thousand?" she crossed her fingers hoping that her man had about a hundred g's to take care of them.

Divine started laughing. "Girl, this is three million in cash and over one million in jewelry. So financially, I'm set. The only thing I need is you to share this with."

"Divine, you have me." Brooklyn was beaming.

"I hope so," Divine said as he pulled out an envelop with some documents in it. "Do you know what these are?" Divine asked Brooklyn showing her the documents.

"No, what are they?"

"This is an insurance policy for two million dollars. If anything happens to me, it goes to my daughter and her caretaker which would be you if you were my wife."

Divine pulled out a white gold necklace with a solid white gold key on it.

"This key is to the black box with the jewelry in it and on the back of the key engraved in Arabic is the combination to the safe," Divine said as he put the chain around Brooklyn's neck.

"Divine, I don't know what to say." She touched the pendant with her hand.

"Don't say anything, just be true to me and my daughter and everything is ours," Divine said as he kissed Brooklyn and started sucking on her neck and her breast as his two-way started to vibrate. "Damn! It never fails," Divine said as he looked at his two-way and noticed a number followed by 666. 666 was the number of the building on Hancock that Divine pushed his weight from. The building was his number one source of money. He had to call the number back immediately. Divine never made any type of business calls on his home phone. He only used the cell phone for that because the cell phone that he had was a flipped number. So the calls could never be traced back to him.

"Yo, who's this? Talk to me." He spoke sternly into the horn.

"Yo, Divine, this is Meth. Yo, God, we just seen that nigga Rahmel fucking with them Panamanians from the corner store." Meth was outside looking back and forth waiting for customers.

"Word, that grimy nigga probably trying to get some shit off of them on consignment. Don't even worry about that nigga. Ya heard?"

"Aight, son, but you know I don't trust that old mutha fucka."

"Oh, yeah, most definitely. We *must* keep our eyes on that nigga. And real soon, we're gonna handle them Panamanians.

In just one minute, ya heard?"

"Aight, peace!"

"Aight, one!"

As soon as Divine hung up the phone, he knew that he would have to call China sooner than he thought.

Chapter 10
When Cowards Creep

Two months had passed and Angel hadn't made any progress. Diamond and Shymeek's relationship was gradually becoming what she always wanted with the exception of Shymeek's disappearances every night with the excuse of recording in the studio. Whenever D-Nice would call, Shymeek would go running. D-Nice was Shymeek's rap artist that was originally from Atlanta. He was a light skin, pretty boy type with long silky hair that he wore in a ponytail. Diamond accepted the fact that he was a music producer and that's what he did. Shymeek provided Diamond with everything she needed and wanted, so she played her position. Brooklyn and Divine were engaged to be married, but that wouldn't happen for a couple of years. They were closer than ever. The only time Diamond saw Brooklyn was when Brooklyn visited Angel at the hospital. Since the situation in N.C., they both had been pre-occupied with their new relationships. Brooklyn was looking like a million bucks; Divine was treating her like she was a queen. She was draped in all the latest fashions and she had on a new piece of jewelry every day. Brooklyn was driving around the hood in Divine's 500 Benz, looking like a movie star.

Diamond was also doing well. She had a week to go before she graduated high school. Diamond's plans were to attend community college in the fall. The sex that Shymeek was laying on her was the best that she ever had, so she never second thought if Shymeek was out cheating on her whenever he went on the road with his artist. She figured that she provided him with whatever he needed sexually. Things were going good for her, a little too good. Diamond was happy for what seemed to be the first time in her life. When Brooklyn told her what Divine had done for her as far as the Pop situation went, Diamond was grateful but at the same time, she was disappointed that she wasn't able to kill Pop herself. But Diamond respected Divine for what he did for her and her mother, most of all, what he was doing for her best and only friend besides her mother and Shymeek.

Lately, Diamond had been feeling queasy in her stomach. She feared that she was pregnant. Her menstruation was late and her cycle was never off. Diamond had made an appointment to see her gynecologist at 1 p.m. that day. Shymeek was in Atlanta with D-Nice working on his album. Diamond sat with Angel every day for hours telling her about everything that was going on in her life since she had been in a coma. Although Angel was unresponsive, it gave Diamond some type of closure. The doctors told Diamond that because Angel was still young and healthy, that she should be able to pull through it, but she would need all the support and love from her family. Besides Diamond, Shymeek and Brooklyn, Mrs. Sheena also came to visit Angel on the weekends.

When Pop and Regg were murdered, Mrs. Sheena figured that Diamond had something to do with their murder. Recently, Diamond had been seeing more and more of her father riding around in the hood especially in Bedstuy. She never bothered to make her presence known. Whenever she would see him riding by, she would either duck or hide her face. She hated Rahmel and he was the last person she wanted to deal with. Diamond blamed him for everything that was wrong in their lives.

Rahmel was spending a lot of time with the Panamanians at their store. They were up to something. Divine had put China on Rahmel. Rahmel was tricking thousands on China. China was just waiting for Divine to give her the word and she would gift wrap him and turn him over to Divine and his henchmen. China reported to Divine all of Rahmel's activities involving the Panamanians. She could tell that they were up to something, but they made it their business to never speak around her. So Divine decided to just move on them before they tried or moved on him. Divine called Draz and told him that he had some work for him and Killa.

• • •

Brooklyn and Divine were inseparable. They were the new Bonnie and Clyde. Brooklyn was always a little tomboy growing up, so she was down for whatever. She would kill something for her man. She swore she would hold him down and be by his side regardless to whom or what. She was a rider. And she knew how to handle herself. Being raised in a house with two older brothers gave her an edge. Brooklyn was picking up and dropping off for Divine whenever he couldn't make the run. She was a soldier and Divine was loving it.

When Divine and Brooklyn left the building, Divine told Brooklyn that they had to make one more stop before they went home. Divine had to meet up with Draz and Killa. Divine had to go to Miami to see Raul and he planned on taking Brooklyn with him so she could meet Raul. So if anything were ever to happen to him, Brooklyn could make sure that Raul got all of his money. Rahmel played heavy on Divine's mind. He knew he couldn't trust him; now he had to die. Divine didn't like the fact that he was running around with the cats who were trying to move in on him on the sneak tip. So Rahmel would die with these cowards.

When Brooklyn first heard Divine mention the name Rahmel, she never gave it a second thought that they were talking about the same Rahmel as in Diamond's father. After Divine's meeting with Draz and Killa, they agreed to hook up with China and get on top of the Rahmel situation immediately.

"Yo, boo, we're going to stay at the house in Queens tonight because we have an early morning flight to catch at JFK. Raul is expecting us early. We don't need to bring anything because we'll go shopping while we're out there. We're going to stay down there for a couple of days. Have you ever been to Miami?" Divine asked.

"No, I have never left New York. But I do know this, that wherever I go, as long as I'm with you, it's going to be a beautiful place," Brooklyn said and smiled.

"So you're down?" Divine asked Brooklyn as they got into his truck and pulled off.

"I'm with you, Daddy. *I'ma ride with ya, take the stand and lie for ya and if I have to, I'll die for ya.*" Brooklyn said quoting a rap song she remembered as she reclined her seat while Divine guided his H2 through the rain-drenched streets of New York.

When Divine pulled in front of his house in Queens, he had a funny feeling. Something wasn't right. Divine's street senses kicked in. From the corner of his eye he detected some movement from behind a tree. Divine paused and then threw his truck back into drive. As he stepped on the gas, two men came from behind the tree running towards them firing their weapons.

POP, POP, POP, POP, BOOM, BOOM, BOOM, POP, POP, POP, BOOM, BOOM, BOOM!!!

Divine put the pedal to the metal. Glass from the back windshield scattered as the bullets hit the front windshield. Both their ears were ringing from the gunfire and the slugs hitting the truck. Divine pushed Brooklyn's head down and told her to stay low as he drove the big H2 as if it was a little Escort. Brooklyn couldn't believe what just happened or who she just saw shooting at them. Now it all started to come together. The person that Divine was talking about *was* Diamond's father Rahmel. Divine was in deep thought. He couldn't believe that this nigga came to his crib and tried to merk him. "How did this mutha fucka know where I lived?" Divine asked himself. *Damn! I'm slipping. This faggot mutha fucka almost got me.* Divine thought to himself. He wanted to kill Rahmel so bad that he started to shed tears. Divine's thoughts were broken by Brooklyn.

"Daddy, I knew who that was that tried to kill us."

"What?! Where do you know that nigga from?" Divine looked at Brooklyn hoping that she wasn't hiding anything from him.

"Remember I was telling you that Diamond and her mother were abused by her father, and how they had it hard while he drove around chasing young girls in his luxury cars?"

"Yeah, I remember." He glanced back at her.

"That was him. That was Rahmel who was shooting at us, that was Diamond's dad."

"Brooklyn, you have to promise me that you would never tell Diamond what's going on with me and her father. Because after tonight, he's a dead man." Divine weaved through traffic. "We don't have to worry about Diamond. She can't stand her father. She blames all the hell that she and Angel have been through on him. The only person Diamond cares about is Angel and me. And after you handled that cat Pop for her, she has nothing but love for you," Brooklyn said as she shook all of the broken windshield glass out of her hair.

"All that might be true, but he's still her father and you must promise me that you will never tell her about the beef I have with her father."

"Alright, Daddy, you don't have to worry about that. Divine, I know where he lives."

"Word?! That's why I love you. But he'll be dealt with," Divine said as he looked into her eyes. He pulled out his cell phone to get his hit squad ready.

• • •

Meth, lil Remo, Black, Troy and Tec were all standing in front of the building on Hancock. The block was booming and they all stood under the awning to escape the rain. It was raining cats and dogs. All of a sudden, everyone immediately stopped what they were doing and stared at two fast approaching SUVs that were speeding toward them. Tec, Black and lil Remo all pulled out their guns on impulse. As the first SUV passed them, the second one came to a full stop. The doors swung open and two men wearing black masks jumped out with AKs and started barking.

BOOM, BOOM, BOOM, BOOM, BOOM, BOOM, BOOM, BOOM, BOOM, BOOM!!!

BUNG...BUNG, BUNG, BUNG, BUNG, BUNG, BUNG, BUNG, BUNG, BUNG!!!

The first ten slugs tore Meth apart and Troy's face

exploded. Black, Tec and Remo ran behind a parked car and fired back.

POP, POP, POP, POP!! BOOM, BOOM, BOOM!! POP, POP, POP, POP, POP, POP!!!

When Remo ran out of bullets, he went into the garbage can and came up with the sawed off shotgun and ran toward the two cats firing.

DOOM...DOOM, DOOM!!
POP, POP, POP, POP, POP, POP, POP, POP!!!!

It sounded like the 4th of July. The AK continued to rip everything that it hit as the two cats that were firing the AKs jumped into the SUV and the driver pulled off. Tec and Black ran behind the SUV still firing at the truck. Once the SUV turned the corner, Black, Tec and lil Remo ran into the building and out the back way into the rear yard. They jumped over a fence into another back yard and came out on Halsey Street where they had their cars parked.

"Yo, is everybody alright?" Black asked as he started up the car and pulled off.

"Yo, who the fuck was that? Did anybody see any of their faces?" Remo asked. He was looking around to see if anyone was following them.

"Nah, son, I was too busy trying to duck them AK slugs," Tec said as he grabbed his ankle.

"Yo, Tec, you aight?" Remo asked.

"Yeah, I think I sprained my ankle when I jumped over that fucking fence in the back yard."

"Man, Meth and Troy never had a chance. Yo, Black, pass me your cell phone so I can call Divine." Remo reached for the phone.

• • •

The doctor told Diamond that she was six weeks pregnant. The doctor advised Diamond to start prenatal care as soon as possible. Diamond was in shock. She wanted to have Shymeek's child, but she had so much that she wanted to accomplish, like college. At the same time, she was pleased to be having Shymeek's seed. It was the only way she knew to pay him back for all he had done for her. A son would be the perfect thank you. Shymeek wouldn't be back until Sunday, That was damn near a week away. She didn't want Shymeek to be the last one to know, but she had to tell somebody her good news. Diamond called Brooklyn, but as usual, she wasn't home. *I'll drop by Brooklyn's house later to see why all of a sudden she's a stranger. But first I know who'll be happy to hear my good news—my mother,* Diamond thought to herself as she headed for the hospital to see Angel.

As Diamond reached Angel's room, the doctors were rushing in and out of her room. Diamond panicked. "Oh, no, what's wrong? What's going on?" Diamond asked as she started running towards Angel's hospital bed.

A short, chubby West Indian lady who was a nurse pulled Diamond's arm and told her that Angel had moved and that Angel was coming out of her coma. "Just have a seat and as soon as the doctors are finished, we will come and get you. So please, just stay calm and relax yourself until the doctors come and speak with you," said the nurse. She went back into the room.

This was too good to be true. This had to be a dream. Shit was going too well to be real. First Diamond found out that she was having a baby by a man who saved her life and now her mother, who meant the world to her, had moved after being in a coma for over two months. Diamond took a seat, folded her hands and said a silent prayer for her mother. In all of

Diamond's life she never really believed in any type of God outside of herself. But after all the events of her life that she had overcome and the obstacles that at times seemed so unbearable and yet she was still alive, healthy and strong, she was convinced that it had to be something out there that was greater than she was that looked over her. So she prayed for her mother. Diamond was a wreck from the anticipation. The doctors were taking for what seemed to be a lifetime to come out of Angel's room with answers.

Fifteen minutes later, the same nurse that told her about Angel coming out of her coma came out of Angel's room with the biggest smile in the world. Diamond looked at the nurse and immediately started crying. The nurse walked up to Diamond and gave her a hug and told her the second greatest news she had in years.

"You are Diamond, I presume," The nurse said. She was holding onto both of Diamond's hands.

"Yes, I am," Diamond answered nervously.

"Your mother wants to see her jewel. She's conscious and you were the first name she asked for." The nurse smiled and allowed Diamond to see her mother.

Diamond ran into Angel's hospital room. When she entered the room, Angel was still hooked up to all of the machines but it was only to monitor her vital signs. Diamond walked up to the bed where a doctor was standing reading a chart and asking Angel a few questions about how she felt. As Diamond walked closer to the bed, they both looked at each other and started crying. These were tears of joy.

Diamond rushed to her mother. They hugged and kissed each other as they cried. They were all they had and they cherished that love. The doctor told Angel that he would be back later. He left so they could be alone.

Diamond had filled her mother in on all the things that had taken place in her life. She told her about Brooklyn and Divine being engaged and then told her about Shymeek moving them into his house. Diamond also told her mother that Brooklyn's man took care of Pop and Regg.

"Mom, you would never have to worry about them hurting you again because they're dead." Diamond told Angel what had happened to Big Ben and how Shymeek came and got her. "And last but not least...," Diamond said as she paused to let everything that she had told her mother sink in. She then told Angel that she would soon be a grandmother. Angel wasn't able to do too much speaking and talking because she was still weak, but that was alright because Diamond did most of the talking. As tears rolled down Angel's face, she whispered to Diamond that she loved her. Before they knew it, visiting hours were up. Diamond kissed Angel on the forehead and told her that she'd be back the following day when visiting hours began.

Diamond left the hospital full of joy and life. She felt that her life was finally coming together. In a couple of weeks, she would be graduating from school, and if all went well, her mother would be attending. She had a good man who loved her and she was bearing their life. To Diamond, nothing could go wrong for her.

Since Shymeek was in Atlanta, she didn't want to go to that big empty house by herself. So she decided to go to Brooklyn's house. She had been trying to reach Brooklyn all day. She had to let her best friend know all the good news she had.

As Diamond left the hospital, she jumped into Shymeek's Range and drove to Brooklyn's house.

Chapter 11

Crossing Over

Divine pulled up and Kyzm, Draz, Killa and Young Soldier were all standing in front of the store on Jefferson Avenue. Young Soldier was another one of Divine's lieutenants. He ran the coke spot in east New York for Divine. Young Soldier was the eighteen-year-old son of Wonderful's baby mother. So in all actuality, Young Soldier was the older brother of Divine's nephew, Tyleek. Divine and Young Soldier were tight, so when Divine was put on, he made sure he surrounded himself with people he could trust with his life. Since Wonderful's death, Divine did whatever he could to help out Medina and lil Wonderful. When Wonderful first got with Medina, Young Soldier was eight years old and always stayed in some shit. Wonderful had given him the name Young Soldier because although he couldn't fight for damn, he never hesitated nor did he ever back down from problems. He was always quick to handle his business. His boxing skills were suspect, but once he had a gun in his hand, Young Soldier was a champion.

Divine had called them all from his cell phone and told them to meet him at the store. He gave them a brief synopsis of what had gone down without getting too deep into details over the phone. Divine had tried to reach Meth numerous times but was unsuccessful. As Divine and Brooklyn got out of the truck, Divine looked at his shit in disbelief. The H2 had over twenty holes in it. It was amazing that neither he nor Brooklyn got hit. "That nigga got to die!" Divine said out loud as they all surrounded the truck.

"Brooklyn, I want you to go to your crib and I'll come get you when I finish here. I'll be there in a few. We're still going to Miami tomorrow. I have to make this trip. It's real important," Divine said to Brooklyn as he turned to Kyzm. "Yo, Ky, let her use your car."

Kyzm gave Brooklyn the keys to his 745il with no second thoughts.

"I'll be there in a little while," Divine told Brooklyn as he kissed her. She jumped into the Beamer and pulled off.

As Divine walked back over to where they were standing, his two-way went off. 666 911911911911.

"Yo, that's the building. Something must've happened. They're hitting my hip like crazy," Divine said as they all walked into the store and headed straight for the back room.

Lil Mike was working the spot. It was his shift. He had a lil shorty with him who was rolling up a blunt.

"Yo, lil Mike, close the store for the rest of the night," Kyzm said as he followed Divine and them to the back.

As soon as everyone entered the room, Divine closed the door and told Young Soldier to try and call Meth and them back at the building. After numerous unsuccessful tries to reach Meth, Soldier decided to call lil Remo's cell.

"Remo, what's up? What's poppin'?" Young Soldier asked. He felt relieved when he heard Remo's voice.

"Yo, son, shit's hectic. Niggas came through and shot up the block. Meth and Troy are dead."

"What?! Yo, who?! Did y'all see any faces? Do y'all know who did it?" Young Soldier's heart started racing.

"Nah, niggas rolled up and jumped out of a truck with masks on and started hitting at us with AKs. We hit up the truck but we don't know if we hit anybody," Remo explained.

"What about the building and the work?" Soldier asked as he looked at Divine.

"All of that is safe. We locked up the apartments and shut down all operations."

"Yo, it was that nigga Rahmel and the Panamanians. They just tried to hit Divine at his crib. We're all at the spot on Jefferson."

"What?!! We're on our way," Remo said looking at the crew he had with him.

"Aight, one!"

"One!"

As soon as Soldier hung up his phone, Divine told him to call China and to tell her to come over to Jefferson immediately.

• • •

When Diamond pulled up in front of Brooklyn's house, a money green BMW pulled up behind her. Diamond couldn't see who was driving the car because the heavy rain made it impossible for her to see anything out the back windshield through the rearview mirror. She noticed Brooklyn jump out and run to her porch to escape the rain.

"Bitch! Who's Beamer you're driving?" Diamond screamed as she got out the truck and ran to the house behind Brooklyn.

"Girl, what are you doing out here in all this damn rain? Why your ass ain't home getting some dick from that fine ass nigga of yours?" Brooklyn asked as she opened the front door.

"I've been trying to catch up with your ass, Bitch. Where

have you been? Somewhere all up that rich nigga's ass?" Diamond said as they both laughed.

"That's right, bitch, you better say it. Holla!" Brooklyn said, taking off the wet clothes she had on as soon as she entered the house.

Brooklyn had no shame of her body. She knew that she looked good. Besides, Diamond had seen her naked plenty of times, not to mention the one time that they had their girl-to-girl moment. As Diamond looked at Brooklyn's naked body, she noticed that she had put on a couple of pounds.

"Divine got me head over heels on him. That nigga is rocking my world and he spoils me. Girl, I'm never gonna let that nigga out of my sight and I'ma throw this thing on him every chance I get," Brooklyn said as she pulled her robe from off of the bathroom's door.

"Brooklyn, guess what!" Diamond teased.

"What?" Brooklyn stopped what she was doing and eyed her friend.

"I'm pregnant!"

"What?! Bitch, don't play with me." Brooklyn leaned her weight to her right side, placed her hands on her hips, wiggled her neck and rolled her eyes playfully.

"Girl, I'm serious. I went to the doctor today. I am a little over five weeks pregnant." Diamond smiled.

"Girl, you serious?"

"Hoe, yeah, I'm serious." Diamond rolled her eyes back at her friend.

Brooklyn hugged Diamond and started screaming. "Aaahh! Bitch, that better not be that fat mutha fucka's baby," Brooklyn said as she quickly stopped jumping around.

"Bitch, hell no. Ben never got the pleasure to feel these walls with his sour smelling dick. And besides that, I'm not even six weeks yet and Ben has been dead over two months."

"Girl, I'm happy for that. I wouldn't want my goddaughter looking like that mutha fucka. Did you tell Shymeek yet?"

"Not yet, he's in Atlanta working on D-Nice's album. I've only told one other person besides you."

"Bitch, who else you told? I'm the only friend you have. Nobody else wanna be around your trifling ass. So who could you have told besides me and Shymeek?" Brooklyn went back into her ghetto stance with her arms crossed this time.

"Brooklyn, guess what?"

"What?!!"

"Mommy came out of her coma today while I was there visiting her. She's doing real good."

"Diamond, for real?" Brooklyn said and hugged Diamond again. They both started shedding tears of joy.

• • •

"Damn! Fuck! We missed the bastard. That mutha fucka must've had a guardian angel looking over his mutha fucking shoulders. Fuck!" Rahmel and his female companion ran back to their car that he had parked down the block from Divine's house in the cut.

"Yo, China, this shit is fucked up. That nigga seen my face."

"Daddy, I told you to wear a mask. You don't like to listen, Daddy," China said as she pulled off the mask she wore to conceal her face.

"Damn! We fucked up. I got to kill that nigga," Rahmel said as he pounded the palm of his hand on the steering wheel.

"Don't worry about it, Daddy. We still have the edge, remember. He paid me to set you up. He still thinks that I'm going to set you up for him. I had a mask on so he didn't see my face. I bet he's going crazy trying to find out how you found out where he lives. I know it never crossed his mind that I would flip on him. Me and my girls have put plenty of work in for him. So he trusts me. He would never figure it out and if he did, by that time, it would have been too late for him. So try to calm down, Daddy, we have the edge. Loosen up, you're too tense. As a matter of fact, I know how to loosen you up," China said as she leaned over and unzipped Rahmel's pants. She proceeded to give Rahmel some brains while he carefully drove the stolen van through the rainy wet streets of Queens headed back to Brooklyn.

China was to gain Rahmel's trust and confidence so when the time came and Divine gave her the word, she would be his key to Rahmel. But evidently, things didn't go as he planned. Rahmel was a cultivator. He knew the art of manipulation. He played on the minds of people. He made it his business to break the so-called strong-minded. And with China, he put his work in. He told the women what they wanted to hear. He would wine and dine them with all of the luxuries and dreams of a baller lifestyle. Not to mention that his tongue game was his sword, in the bed and verbally. Rahmel splurged his money on China. Rahmel was experienced and an older man, so his wisdom on the game and life intrigued her. China slowly but surely started to fall for Rahmel's game. Rahmel was a womanizer, so he knew all the right things to say and do to captivate a woman's mind and heart. The last couple of weeks that China was around Rahmel, she started to believe his game and promises. He charmed her, and eventually China broke down and told Rahmel Divine's plans on moving on him. Rahmel fucked and ate China's pussy so good that she broke down and told him everything. How she and her girls used to set rival dealers up for Divine and even told Rahmel where Divine lived in Queens. China had switched sides. China was only loyal to the almighty dollar. And Rahmel made her better promises than the couple of g's that Divine was paying her. She was loyal to whoever was talking the biggest dollar signs. Divine had more money by far, but Divine wasn't trying to come off of any of it. Besides that, China knew her dreams of ever becoming Divine's girl were dead. He had his new young girl who Divine gave the world to. China felt that it should have been her. She hated whenever she saw the two of them together. So this played a major part in her decision to switch to what she assumed to be a winning team.

Chapter 12
A Night To Remember

After Diamond left the hospital from visiting Angel, she was in good spirits. Angel had made tremendous progress over the last twenty-four hours. The doctors said that Angel was an amazing person, that they had never witnessed anyone with her will and desire to live. Angel had all of her strength and was able to talk when just twenty-four hours ago she was in a comatose state. Angel informed Diamond that she had remembered every visit. "I was conscious but my body wouldn't respond," Angel said as she started crying. "I wanted to reach out to you but I couldn't."

The doctors said that this was normal for people who were in a comatose state because their minds were still active. That's why it's very important that the families come and sit with the patients and talk with them and show them that support. The one thing that Angel had on her side was that she was still young and healthy. The doctors would keep her under their care for a couple more weeks to run a series of tests.

Diamond crossed the street headed for the Range she had parked across from the hospital. Diamond wasn't paying attention. Her mind was on the current events surrounding their life that were starting to finally look like it was going well. Diamond reached the Range and put the key into the door when out of nowhere, Diamond's thoughts were broken by an all-black Benz pulling up beside her with all its windows tinted out so you couldn't see in. As the car stopped directly in front of her, the passenger's side window slowly came down. Diamond was shocked. It was Diamond's father, Rahmel. The second thing Diamond noticed was the half Asian girl that was driving who couldn't be much older than herself. Rahmel was reclined back in his seat like he was the man.

"Looks like you're doing pretty good for yourself," Rahmel said as he looked at the chrome rims on the Range. "What nigga's dick you're sucking that let you drive his truck?"

Diamond was in shock that she was talking to her estranged father after the last three years of her and Angel ducking and hiding from him. Diamond looked into his eyes and she could feel the hatred in her heart start to come over her. Besides the years of the streets starting to take its hold on him, Diamond was the female image of her father. She didn't even acknowledge the comment that came out of is mouth.

"Huh! What?" Diamond responded in disbelief to Rahmel's question.

"You heard me, if you can, huh, you can hear? So you and Angel think y'all can hide forever? Brooklyn ain't big enough, remember that. I'm gonna find y'all and tell that no-good mother of yours when I do I haven't forgotten what she did. I got something for her ass." Rahmel rolled his window up and china pulled off.

Diamond couldn't believe that the nigga had the nerve to come out his face. After three years of not being there and fifteen years of abuse, all he could say and do was send threats to her mother. *My mother was almost murdered and this bitch ass nigga sending threats to her. Fuck that pussy, woman beating nigga,* Diamond sat in the truck and thought to herself before she pulled off. *Fuck Rahmel. Let me go spend some of Shymeek's money to get my mind off of that no-good nigga. This bitch don't even know that my mother is up in the hospital and that she just came out of a coma. If that nigga ever touch my mother again, I'll kill him myself.* Diamond headed for the Fulton Street mall.

It was 2 a.m. in the morning and Diamond was awakened by the sound of keys in the door. Immediately she got excited. She knew it was Shymeek because nobody else had the house keys. Diamond had been so very lonely the last couple of days. Her pregnancy had her hormones going crazy. Sex was on her mind all of the time lately. She had masturbated more times in that week than she had her whole entire life. When Shymeek entered the bedroom, she could tell that he was pissy drunk.

Shymeek walked up to the bed and started undressing, then got into the bed with Diamond. Shymeek didn't say a word; he just started licking on Diamond's neck while he fingered Diamond's vagina. Shymeek was drunk and sloppy, but Diamond didn't care because she had been yearning for his touch all week. Shymeek loved the fact that Diamond allowed him to do whatever he wanted and whatever turned him on to her. She was his sex slave. Shymeek palmed Diamond's breast roughly as he sucked and nibbled on her nipples. Diamond stared at the ceiling and tried to ignore the smell of alcohol on Shymeek's breath.

"Come on, Daddy, I need you inside of me now," Diamond said as her insides were yearning to be pleasured by his manhood.

Shymeek picked Diamond's legs up and bent them over

and pinned them behind her head, giving him leeway to all pussy. He proceeded to lick and suck on Diamond's clit and vaginal walls forcefully. Diamond grinded her hips to Shymeek's touch. She moaned in ecstasy as Shymeek's tongue darted in and out, up and down, side to side exploring every inch of Diamond's womanhood.

"Oh, yes! Yeah, Shymeek, right there! That's the spot, right there. Yeah, right there! Ohhhh!!!" Diamond was enjoying what Shymeek was doing to her. Although he was a little too rough and drunk, he still knew all the right spots to hit. As Diamond started cumming, Shymeek put his focus back on Diamond's breasts. He licked and sucked one nipple at a time then simultaneously placed them both into his mouth pushing her breasts together as Shymeek penetrated Diamond. Diamond wrapped her legs around Shymeek's waist feeling his shaft pulsating as he hammered her with hard long strokes.

"Oooowww! Yes! Yes! Yeah, right there. I'm cumming!"

Diamond succumbed to Shymeek's hard shaft as he darted in and out. With each thrust into Diamond, he made circular motions as he held his manhood inside of her. After over an hour of passionate "fucking," Shymeek told Diamond that he wasn't through, that he had a surprise for her. He told Diamond to turn over into the doggy position and he started licking on her ass cheeks. Shymeek sucked and licked each cheek and then he proceeded to toss Diamond's salad. Shymeek spread her ass cheeks apart and started licking and tonguing Diamond's asshole. Diamond wiggled and grinded her hips to Shymeek's tongue. He dictated her motion with his tongue. Diamond was gone; she was in a state of ecstasy. At the same time that Shymeek licked and sucked Diamond's ass tunnel, he played with her clit bringing Diamond to another orgasm. Diamond's body shook uncontrollably as she came. She fell forward and laid on her stomach. Shymeek continued to lick and suck all over Diamond. Shymeek was in rare form that evening. He licked Diamond from the back of her neck to the bottom of her feet. He stopped at her feet and sucked Diamond's toes. This sent chills up her body. Shymeek was stimulating parts of her body that she didn't know could be stimulated. *Shymeek might not have produced any platinum records yet, but he sure had a platinum tongue game. And with that, he'd get producer of the year from me any day,"* Diamond thought to herself as they laid in each other's arms savoring the moment. Eventually they drifted off to sleep.

That next morning, Diamond told Shymeek of her mother's recovery and how she saw her father and the foul shit that he said to her.

"Don't even worry about that cat, Diamond. It's about you and me," Shymeek said as he sat up in the bed and started rolling a blunt.

"Baby, I have something else to tell you."

"What's that, baby girl?" Shymeek licked the blunt so that it could seal shut.

"I went to the doctor the other day because I wasn't feeling good and I took a pregnancy test."

"And?" He looked up at her.

"I'm pregnant!"

"What? Stop playing." Shymeek put the blunt down.

"For real, baby. We're having a little son or daughter." Tears were forming in her eyes.

"Girl, that's the greatest thing that could ever happen to us. Girl, I love you!" Shymeek said as he put the blunt down that he had in his hand and grabbed Diamond and stuck his tongue in her mouth.

They made love and stayed in the bed all day. They would

go visit Angel that evening. Right then, it was all about them.

• • •

Divine had gotten in touch with China. Rahmel dropped China off and she met up with Divine and them at the store. China never knew of this spot, which is why Rahmel and them didn't hit this spot. But once she got back, she would inform him. China agreed to set Rahmel up for Draz and Killa to hit Rahmel in a hotel. But the only problem was that China no longer was loyal to Divine's team. So instead of setting Rahmel up, she would flip it and Draz and Killa would be the ones getting set up. Divine had to leave for Miami in the morning but everybody knew what had to be done. Kyzm, Young Soldier and Black were to move all the work out of the building on Hancock to a warehouse on Lexington Avenue. But Divine was slipping because he revealed all his plans to his crew in front of China. China sat back and took in all of the information so she could report it back to Rahmel. The setup was set for the following day and Kyzm was to move all the work from the building by eight in the morning. Divine had just received 500 keys from Raul's people a couple of days ago. Divine had half of Raul's money that he wanted to give him which was the reason for his and Brooklyn's trip to Miami. Divine left China Draz' cell phone number and told him that she would call him the following night when everything was a go. China told them that Rahmel was into doing freaky shit, so she would handcuff him to the bed while Draz and Killa waited downstairs until she would page them. Once they received her page, it meant that she was ready for them to come up and get their man. Everybody agreed with the plan and China left.

Damn! These niggas don't even know what's going on. These young punks don't even have a clue. Rahmel better hit me off good for this one, China thought to herself as she left the store and caught a cab to her crib where Rahmel was waiting.

• • •

As soon as China reached her apartment, she told Rahmel word for word details of everything that was spoken about at the meeting with Divine and his crew. She made sure she told him about Kyzm moving the work to a warehouse on Lexington and that they had expected for her to set it up to get him at a hotel that evening so that Draz and Killa would be able to come and hit him up. China even let Rahmel know about the spot on Jefferson and Broadway.

"You did good, baby," Rahmel said as he stuck his tongue into China's mouth. "This is what I want you to do. Call them niggas and tell them that everything is a go for tomorrow night. And as for the warehouse, I have a surprise for them," Rahmel said as he took out his cell and called Alfonso.

While Rahmel spoke on the phone, China slowly and provocatively undressed in front of Rahmel. All of this made her juices start to flow. She was feeling horny. She wanted to fuck. China bent down and knelt in front of Rahmel while he was talking on the phone. She unzipped his pants, pulled out his manhood and took him into her mouth.

• • •

When Divine and Brooklyn exited the plane in Miami's airport, Raul had a limo waiting for their arrival. About an hour later, the limo was pulling up to Raul's secluded fenced off Miami beach villa. Two armed Columbians, who Divine recognized as Raul's personal security, approached the limo. They looked into the limo and gave Divine a head nod and told the driver to proceed. One of the guards spoke into his walkie talkie and the gate automatically parted. The driveway from the gate to the front of the house was about a half of a mile. When the limo pulled up in front of the actual villa, Raul was sitting out by the pool with two young Columbian girls who couldn't be any older than eighteen. The weather in Miami and New York was as different as night and day. When they left New York, it was rainy and a little chilly, but Miami was hot and humid. When Divine and Brooklyn got out of the limo, Raul got up to meet them followed by his two goddesses.

"Divine, my most trusted friend," Raul said as he extended his hand and gave Divine a hug. "This must be the beautiful young lady you have been telling me about." Raul grabbed Brooklyn's hand and kissed it. "I'm Raul," he said in a complimenting manner.

"Nice to finally meet you, Raul. I have heard so much about you as well. I'm Brooklyn." She smiled showing her pearly whites.

"Oh, and these are my two assistants," Raul said introducing the two young ladies he was with. The females had on thongs and were topless. "How was y'all's flight?" he asked.

"Laid back, baby. When we left New York, it was coming down. We get out here and it's like another world," Divine said looking around.

"Divine, did you bring that?" Raul asked. It was time to get down to business.

"You know I did. I like to keep all of our business straight before I do anything. It's in the suitcases in the trunk."

"Well, come in and join me in the house." Raul hit both the girls on the ass and told them to get the suitcases out of the trunk as he lead Divine and Brooklyn into the house.

Divine's dick got hard as he watched both girls' asses wiggle when Raul smacked them both on the butt. As they walked to the limo to get the suitcases, Divine fantasized about having a threesome with the girls and he knew if he didn't have Brooklyn with him, Raul would have made that possible for him. Brooklyn gave Divine a look as if to say *you better not even think about it*. They then followed Raul into the villa.

Chapter 13
The Takeover

Rahmel watched from a roof a couple of buildings down as Kyzm, Black and Young Soldier loaded a U-Haul truck with the boxes of coke. As soon as they finished loading the U-Haul, Black and Soldier jumped into the truck while Kyzm jumped into a Durango. When Kyzm pulled off, Black followed.

Rahmel called his people that he had awaiting his call close by. "Yo, they're making a move. There's a red Durango in front of them. That's that cat Kyzm. He's with them," Rahmel said into his walkie talkie. As they made a left turn on Patchen and Hancock, Rahmel's people spotted the truck and made their move.

WHOOP! WHOOP!

"Oh shit, son! The police are behind us flashing their lights," Black said as he reached for the gun he had on the seat next to him. "Yo, son, I'm not letting them pigs take me in with all this shit in the back of the truck."

"Yo, son, calm down. Don't panic. All the paperwork for this fucking truck is legit, right? Do you have your license?" Young soldier asked.

"Yeah, no doubt, everything is on the up and up," Black

answered.

"Aight then, we shouldn't have anything to worry about. Just play it cool. Pull over and see what they want. If shit don't look good, we'll give it to them. Ya heard?" Young Soldier suggested.

As Black pulled the U-Haul over, Kyzm pulled over in front of them. Black noticed another police patrol car pull up. Kyzm watched from his car trying to see what was going on. He saw that the police car that pulled the truck over had two black police in it. In the other there were two black or Hispanic officers. The two black officers walked to the truck. As the police approached the truck, Black rolled his window down.

"Good morning, Officer, may I help you?" Black asked carefully.

"License and registration, sir," the officer requested.

"Officer, what seems to be the problem?" Black asked as he passed all the papers to the truck and his license to the officer.

"Nothing major. You just made an illegal turn back on Patchen. Just sit tight and if all your papers are correct, I'll just write you a ticket and y'all can be on y'all's way," the officer said as he walked back to his car with the other officer.

"Yo, son, I told you. You can't be so quick to react without feeling out the situation first. You would've gotten us into a whole heap of shit if you would have started blasting," Soldier said as he sat back and awaited the officer's return with the ticket.

"Here they come now, son. That shit was quick," Soldier said looking through his side view mirror.

"Yeah, let us get our shit so we can keep it moving. We got drugs to sell," Soldier said as they both laughed.

As both officers approached the vehicle, one came around

to the passenger side and the other walked to Black's side while Black rolled his window down.

"Is everything alright, sir?" Black asked.

"Yes, I have a ticket here for you making an illegal turn. Pay the ticket and everything will be okay." The officer gave Black the ticket and told him to drive safely.

"Alright, Officer, will do," Black said as he bent over to put the registration in the truck's glove compartment. When Black looked back up, the officer had a 44 caliber with a silencer on it pointed at his head. That's when Black knew that they weren't real police.

Sssspit, pit, pit, pit pit!!!

Black's blood, brain and skull fragments hit Soldier as he reached for Black's gun under the seat. The officer that was standing on *his* side took aim.

Sssspit, pit, pit, pit, pit!!!

Kyzm watched what happened from his truck and froze from the shock. By the time he snapped out of it, two heavily armed men were running towards his truck firing at him.

BLATTA...BLATTA, BLATTA, BLATTA!!!!!

The slugs ripped through the Durango tearing into Kyzm's flesh. The two men ran up to the truck and they both fired into Kyzm's window hitting him in the face and head, making sure he was dead.

BLATTA...BLATTA!!!!!!!

They ran and jumped into the squad cars while the men dressed in the police uniforms pushed Black and Soldier's bodies out of the truck, jumped in and pulled off with Divine's truck full of coke.

• • •

"Shymeek, after I leave the hospital, I'ma go to the apartment on Bergen Street to collect all of my mother's things. Can I use the truck?" Diamond asked.

"Yeah, D-Nice is coming to get me. We have to go to Def Jam's office. What time do you think you'll be home?" Shymeek questioned.

"I should be finished no later than 1 a.m. Mrs. Sheena from next door said that she would help me. I tried to call Brooklyn, but I forgot that she and Divine were going to Miami this morning."

"Diamond, as soon as you finish, call me. I'm going to need you to come and get me, aight?"

"Sure will, Daddy." Diamond gave Shymeek a kiss and was out the door.

Fifteen minutes later, Diamond was entering the hospital to see Angel. When Diamond entered Angel's room, Angel was sitting up watching TV.

"Hey, beautiful, look at you," Diamond said as she gave Angel a hug. Diamond still couldn't believe that over forty-eight hours ago Angel was in a coma.

"Girl, I hope you brought me some real food. I'm starving. It's time for me to start gaining my weight back. Girl, I done lost all of my shape. I'm all bones. Girl, look at me, I lost all my ass," Angel said as she stood up and tried to look at her butt.

"Ma, don't even worry about that. You'll gain it all back and then some as soon as we get you home. You're looking real good for someone who was just in a coma. Oh yeah, ma, after the visit I'm going to the apartment to pack all of your stuff and move them to Shymeek's house."

"Diamond, I don't now about moving in on you and Shymeek and invading y'all's space and privacy."

"Ma, don't talk crazy. It's always been about you and me. It will always be like that. Before there was Shymeek *and* after

Shymeek. Now come on and let me do something to all that pretty hair that you have. It's a mess." Diamond stood over Angel as she sat in her chair watching TV and started braiding her hair.

Diamond corn-rolled Angel's hair in a style while they talked about everything. Angel broke down and told Diamond about her brief addiction to crack and how she used to have sex with Pop to support her addiction. They both held each other and cried. Angel promised that she was through getting high. Diamond told Angel everything she used to do with Big Ben and for Big Ben. Diamond told Angel how much money she had saved and about the money she took off of Ben's body when he was shot.

"Ma, I have a surprise for you." Diamond pulled out the box that she took off of Ben when he was murdered and gave it to Angel.

Angel opened the box and her eyes almost popped out of her head. She couldn't believe the size of the diamond on the ring. "Diamond, it's beautiful and it's so big."

"Yeah, my name is Diamond, but you are my diamond; *A Diamond in the Rough.*"

They both hugged each other and started crying again. Their love for one another was unconditional.

"Baby, everything is going to be alright. We're going to make it," Angel said as she wiped her and Diamond's tears with her hospital gown.

Visiting hours were up and Diamond gave her mother a kiss and told her that she would see her the next day. Once Diamond left the hospital and got into the truck, she noticed that she had left the keys to the apartment on Bergen at the house and that she had left her cell phone.

"Damn! I can't believe I left them damn keys and my cell

phone. If my head wasn't connected to my body, I might have left that. Now I have to go all the way back to the house and then come back this way to go to Bergen Street. Damn!" Diamond said to herself as she started up the Range and pulled off.

• • •

After Divine and Brooklyn left Raul's villa, they got a hotel suite on the beach. Divine had given Raul 1.125 million which was half of what he owed Raul for the 500 keys. Now it was time for him and Brooklyn to enjoy their vacation. Divine tried to clear his mind of that nigga Rahmel trying to hit him and Brooklyn. By the time they get back to New York, Draz, Killa and China should have handled the Rahmel situation. Kyzm and Soldier would keep everything as far as the work *and* the spots running smoothly. The work basically sold itself.

It was nighttime and the weather in Miami was beautiful. Divine and Brooklyn lay on the beach talking and looking up at the clear sky enjoying each other's company.

"Daddy, do you know that these last couple of months I have had were the greatest times of my life? You have brought so much joy and foreclosure into my world. And no one ever showed me the love I've received from you. I want to spend the rest of my life with you. Divine, I'll give my life for you. Do you know as children, Diamond and I used to fantasize about our prince charmings coming and sweeping us off our feet. Are you that prince charming?" Brooklyn asked as she gazed into the clear skies.

"I don't know, ma, let's find out," Divine said as he turned over on top of Brooklyn and started sucking on her neck.

"Oooooww! Daddy you know that's my spot."

"Yeah, I know, believe me, I know!" Divine said with a

devilish smile on his face. He pulled Brooklyn's bra off and started licking and sucking on her breasts.

"Daddy, what if someone comes and catches us?"

"I hope they enjoy the show. Because I want you right here under the moon and in the sands of Miami. Let's make this a night to remember."

Divine went down on Brooklyn. Brooklyn held her breath as she enjoyed Divine's touch as he tenderly dragged his tongue through the split of her vaginal walls, stopping every so often to dab at her clit with the tip of his tongue. He was sending electrical impulses throughout her entire body.

"Mmmmm," Brooklyn moaned. "Oh, that feels so good, Daddy, ohhh!" Brooklyn was groaning with pleasure.

Divine slid his tongue between the inner lips of Brooklyn's walls as she groaned and rotated her hips in round, small, tight circles.

"Oh, God! Yes!" Brooklyn hissed. "Give it to me, Daddy! Yes! Lick it good for me, Daddy. It's yours. Lick it faster, Daddy, I'm cumming. Aieee! Yes! Ooooh! Yes, Daddy, yes!"

Brooklyn started to shake violently as she hit her peak. Brooklyn sat up and maneuvered herself between Divine's thighs. She grabbed his manhood with a tight solid grip and took him into her mouth deeper and deeper.

"Agggghhh! Yeah!" Divine bellowed. "Right there, that's it! Right there!"

Brooklyn buried her face in between Divine's legs. He bent his knees and held Brooklyn's head between his thighs as he massaged her tits and slightly pinched her stiff nipples. Brooklyn deep throated his manhood. Divine watched Brooklyn's head bob up and down on his cock. Brooklyn had the best head game that Divine had ever had and he had them all. After several minutes of Brooklyn's deep throating, she started licking down his shaft. She stopped at the base and proceeded to suck and lick on his nuts taking them both into her mouth. "Awww! Yes!" Divine squealed in a high-pitched voice.

Brooklyn felt Divine's cock start pulsating as if he was ready to cum, so she stopped and looked into his eyes provocatively. "Come on, Daddy, I want your manhood inside of me."

Brooklyn laid back and spread her legs and let Divine part the lips of her walls. He guided the head of his throbbing cock into the hot, wet depths of Brooklyn's insides. "Mmmm. Yeah, Daddy, right there." Brooklyn laid back as Divine held her thighs and began to thrust himself inside of her. He slammed his manhood all the way in until he couldn't go any further and he started grinding hard short strokes. Divine held Brooklyn's legs closer together as she tucked her knees against her breasts. Rhythmically, she met each of Divine's thrusts with one of her own. "Mmmm, yes, Daddy! Yeah, right there. Ohhh! Gawwwwd! Yes, Divine! Yes!" The more Brooklyn would moan, the harder and faster Divine would thrust and the deeper he tried to go. As both of them reached their climax, Divine heard somebody coming. He looked up and another couple was walking towards them with their beach towel and radio in their hands.

"Oh, shit, baby. Somebody's coming," Divine said as he rolled off of Brooklyn and started putting on his shorts. Brooklyn started getting dressed. They both laughed as the couple walked by. "I see that we weren't the only ones with love on our minds," the man said to his girl as they walked by.

"Come on, Daddy, let's go back to the room and finish where we left off," Brooklyn said to Divine as they finished getting dressed.

As soon as they entered the room, Divine's two-way was

going off. Divine grabbed it off the table where he had left it and noticed it was the building.

"Why the fuck are they paging me from the building? They should have shut all operations down at the building already. There should be no reason for them to be there right now," Divine said as he passed Brooklyn the blunt off the table with some weed and picked up his cell phone.

"Yo, Kyzm, this is Divine. What's up?" Divine angrily spat into the phone.

"Yo, Divine, this is lil Remo." Remo sounded weird.

"Remo, what's up?"

"Yo, God, they murdered Kyzm, Black and Soldier. And they took the truck of coke."

"WHAT?!?" Divine couldn't believe what he just heard.

"Yo, I've been trying to reach you all day. Niggas were dressed up like the police and pulled them over when they were moving the coke. They murdered them and then took the truck."

"Where's Draz and Killa?"

"I paged them numerous times and they haven't gotten back at me."

"Remo, I'll be there in the morning. Get everybody off the streets and have them meet me at the house in Queens."

"Aight, peace."

"One."

As Divine hung up the phone, he looked at Brooklyn in disbelief. "How could somebody know about the move? It had to come from inside," Divine thought to himself. Divine picked up the phone to call Raul. He had over two hundred keys in that truck. He would pay Raul out of his own pocket, but as of now, he was out of work and he would mark that off as a loss. But you better believe, somebody was gonna answer for his loss.

• • •

At 10 p.m. that night, China paged Killa and told him at which hotel she and Rahmel were, and that she would call them back in about an hour when she had him nice and drunk. Forty-five minutes later, Draz and Killa were down in the parking lot of the hotel waiting for China's call.

"Yo, son, that's that nigga Rahmel's Lex right there," Killa said as he spotted Rahmel's car.

"Yeah, that nigga won't be driving that pretty mutha fucka anymore. Ya heard?" Draz stated.

"Damn! They've been paging me from the building all day."

"Yeah, me too. But I'm focused on what we are here to do. That's why I turned my shit off. As long as yours is on, China can reach us. Don't worry about them at the building right now. When we call them back, we'll have some good info for them."

• • •

"Yo, Dog, y'all niggas ready?" Rahmel asked his associates.

"Yeah, Rahmel, let's get this party started," one of them answered fingering the trigger of his gun.

"Yo, remember, as soon as they enter the room, air them niggas out and keep it moving. No fuck ups. We have the upper hand, so everything should run smoothly. They're not expecting it so we have the jump on them. Me and China will be down the hall in case shit don't go right. I'll catch 'em in the hall if y'all happen to miss them, which y'all shouldn't. After it's all done, everybody meet me back at my storefront in Brownsville. Be ready. As soon as we get to the room, China is gonna page them. They're right downstairs. So as soon as they get her page, that's their cue to make the move."

As soon as Rahmel and China got into their room, China paged Killa...

• • •

"Yo, Draz, that's China. They're in room 112. You ready? Let's go." Killa was ready to kill.

Draz and Killa both put their wigs on and got out of the car. They entered the building through the back and used the back staircase to the third floor. As they walked up to the door, they heard a woman's voice screaming like she was having sex.

"They must be looking at a porno because I know that nigga Rahmel ain't handling his business like that," Killa said to Draz as he turned the doorknob.

As soon as the door opened, they entered with their guns drawn. As they walked in, they froze from surprise. Before they could react, they spotted the flashes before they heard the thunder.

BLATTA! BLATTA, BLATTA, BAM, BAM, BAM. BLATTA, BLATTA!!!

Draz and Killa were dead before they hit the floor. They never knew what hit them. As they dropped to the floor, the two assailants ran out the room.

As soon as Rahmel and China heard the shooting, they left the hotel.

Chapter 14
When The World Comes Crashing Down

When Diamond pulled up in front of the Shymeek's house, all the lights were off. *D-Nice must have come and picked Shymeek up already,* Diamond thought to herself as she got out of the truck and went into the house. When Diamond entered the house, she noticed that the room door was closed and she heard the squeaking sounds of the bed. The same annoying squeaking sounds that the bed made whenever she and Shymeek made love. Diamond walked to the bedroom door and put her ear to the door. She heard what appeared to be moaning and grunts. Diamond's heart dropped to her feet as the thoughts of her knight in shining armor cheating on her with another woman in the same bed that he and she shared. Diamond slowly opened the door.

"Ohh, my God! Noooo!" she screamed.

Diamond slammed the bedroom door in disbelief and ran into the living room. Shymeek heard Diamond scream and jumped up in surprise. He ran out the room behind her. Diamond couldn't believe what she just witnessed. Shymeek had D-Nice bent over in the doggy style position making love to him like he was a woman. Diamond collapsed on the floor in the living room and started crying. Shymeek tried to explain to Diamond that it was nothing like she thought. Shymeek tried to comfort Diamond, but Diamond pushed him off of her and screamed, "Get your hands off of me." Diamond was in shock. "How could you? I'm having your baby. I'm pregnant with your life inside of me," she screamed hysterically.

"Diamond, it's not what it seems or what it looks like." Shymeek was pleading with Diamond.

"Nigga, please, what it look like? Nigga, you had your dick in that mutha fucka's ass. What the fuck you mean it's not what it looks like?" As the words came out of Diamond's mouth, the reality hit her. The nigga she was willing to commit her life to was *A BROTHER ON THE DOWN LOW*.

Diamond ran out the house and jumped in the Range and pulled off.

As Diamond drove, she realized she didn't have anyplace to go. Brooklyn was in Miami with Divine and Angel was in the hospital. Bergen would be the first place Shymeek would come looking for her so Mrs. Sheena's was a no-no. Diamond couldn't believe that this was happening to her. Just when shit looked as if it was finally going the way it should be. The last thing she would have ever thought was that this nigga was a *BOOTY BANDIT, A PUMP WRANGLER, PILLOW BITER, SHIT PUSHER, SWORD SWALLOWER.* As she thought about it, everything started to come into play. Diamond shook her head in disbelief at the very thought of what she had just witnessed.

That's why that nigga was so fascinated with licking, fucking and sucking her ass. Not to mention that every time D-Nice would call, this nigga went running. The nights that he was supposed to be at the studio all night and on tour, he was fucking this bitch ass nigga. Oh, my Gawwwd! What about

AIDS? Diamond started crying once again at the possibility of Shymeek giving her HIV.

Before Diamond knew it she was in New Jersey. So she decided to get a room for the night to try and clear her head.

"I knew my life was going too good lately for it to be true. The sun don't ever shine on my side of the street," Diamond said as she turned off her cell phone and pager. Shymeek had been calling and paging her since she left the house. She didn't want to be bothered with his homo ass. Right then, she wanted to kill him for his betrayal.

• • •

Once Divine and Brooklyn left Raul's villa, he and Brooklyn headed for the airport. Raul agreed to supply Divine with two hundred more keys that he would have to pick up as soon as he got back to New York. Raul had some suppliers that would have a van full of coke waiting for Divine in a warehouse where they manufactured teddy bears. Before Divine and Brooklyn boarded the plane, Divine called lil Remo and told him to meet him at the airport by 2 p.m. which was the time his plane was scheduled to land.

When Divine and Brooklyn exited the airport, lil Remo and Whop were sitting out front in Whop's Lex truck. Whop was lil Remo's older brother. Whop was bubbling in Virginia. He had a mean team who had close to eight bodies in Virginia in the last year. Divine fronted Whop all his work. Divine had put Whop on as well. Divine and Whop went way back to their junior high school days. When lil Remo called his brother and told him what was going down and how niggas were trying to move on Divine, Whop stopped everything he was doing and came back to Brooklyn. When they were younger, Whop and Divine used to run with a crew called the *Low Lifes*. All they wore was Polo gear. The crew was known for boosting. Divine and Whop were the only ones out of the crew that couldn't boost. They made their money the *ski mask* way.

One day while they were on Canal Street with Wonderful and Draz scheming, trying to hit some pockets, Wonderful decided that he wanted to hit a jewelry store. This was during the time when everybody that was somebody had on a big gold rope chain with a dinner plate on it. As they walked by a jewelry store on Canal and Broadway, Wonderful picked up a brick and threw it through the front window of the jewelry store. As the window came crashing down, Draz, Divine, Wonderful and Whop rushed the window snatching all the jewelry they had on display in the window. Divine and Draz watched their backs. As they broke out running, a man walking by tackled Whop to the ground. Divine turned around and noticed Whop on the ground struggling with the man. Divine went back to help Whop. They both beat the shit out of the man but before they knew it, they were surrounded by the police. The police beat the shit out of them and then locked them up. Wonderful and Draz got away and Divine and Whop did a year and a half upstate for robbery and assault. Whop had always respected Divine for not leaving him when he could have gotten away. He felt like he owed Divine for that. So when Remo called and told Whop that somebody had tried to kill Divine, Whop and his stick man, Kali, were on the first thing smoking back to Brooklyn.

Kali was originally from the west coast, but his father's side of the family lived in Brooklyn and he spent most of his summers in Brooklyn as a child. Kali and Whop were close since they were kids. When Kali first visited his grandparents in Brooklyn, he was fighting every day. The other kids from Brooklyn used to try to test him because he was from the west coast. The first person Kali had a fight with was Whop. After that, they became the best of friends. But every summer they were going at each other's throat trying to prove to each other how tough they were. Kali belong to a *Blood* hood in California for some work he put in on some crips. Kali stayed ready to put in work, he was always down for a *187*. So when Whop told him that Divine had some problems, he didn't ask any questions, he just moved out.

"Okay, it's on now," lil Remo said as he jumped out of the truck and gave Brooklyn a hand with her bags. "What's up, Brooklyn? How was your trip?" he asked.

"Peace, Remo. It's was good although it was cut short." She sucked her teeth.

Whop got out of the truck and gave Divine a hug.

"What's up, God? I hear these fools out here are trying to give the God a hard time."

"Yeah, son, you remember that old timer nigga, Rahmel? Yeah, son, that cat is acting up. I got to get this nigga. Speaking of Rahmel, has anybody heard from Draz, Killa or China?" Divine looked around at everyone.

"Nah, I've been paging them cats all night, son. They haven't gotten back at me yet," lil Remo said as he got in the truck and started it up.

"Oh, yo Whop, this is my other half, Brooklyn. Pardon me, man, my mind is on this cat Rahmel," Divine said as he introduced Brooklyn to Whop.

"What's up, Brooklyn? Nice to meet the woman who can finally get my man on lock. How is he treating you? I know he better be taking good care of you," Whop said as he extended his hand.

"Nice to meet you, Whop, and yes, he's taking very good care of me," Brooklyn said as she shook Whop's hand and got in the back of the truck with Divine.

"Yo, Remo, what's the verdict on the Kyzm, Black and Soldier story?"

"Yo, God, the streets is saying that Rahmel had that shit done, him and the Panamanians."

"Son, what I'm trying to figure out is how did anybody know about that move?" Divine asked as he lit the half of blunt that Remo and Whop had in the front ashtray.

"Divine, maybe them niggas saw them loading the truck up with them things."

"Nah, that couldn't be the case. Their move was too well planned out. They ain't just see Kyzm and them loading a U-Haul truck and decide to kill everybody *and* take the truck with the assumption that there were drugs in the truck. They had to know something. That tells me we got someone in the camp that mentioned something to Rahmel."

"The only ones that knew everything were the people that were at the storefront that night. Which was me, you, Black, Kyzm, Soldier, Draz and Killa. And Black, Kyzm and Soldier were killed by the niggas who took the truck and no one's heard from Draz and Killa."

"Yo, what about that bitch China? She was there that night too and we haven't heard from that bitch yet. Draz and Killa should have gotten back with us about that Rahmel situation. You know that bitch is trife. She set up her own baby's father for us, so you know she don't give a fuck about us. And she's been fucking with that nigga, Rahmel, for a couple of weeks now. That nigga Rahmel used to be a pimp, so it wouldn't be too hard for him to flip that bitch's mind with some promises of getting rich," Remo reasoned.

"Word, son, I don't know why I trusted that bitch. Yo, did you tell everybody to meet us at the crib in Queens?" Divine asked.

"Yeah, Kali is at the house with everybody waiting for you," Remo explained.

"Aight, yo, first we have to drop Brooklyn off at the house then we gonna go handle our business. That bitch and her whole family is dying tonight," Divine said as he dialed Raul's suppliers in Queens to let them know that he was on his way. Once they dropped Brooklyn off at her house Divine told Remo to drive to Queens.

• • •

Diamond slept through the night. When she got up it was after two in the afternoon. Diamond checked her pager and it was full to capacity with Shymeek's house number. She wasn't ready to speak to him. She had to process everything before she could face him again. As a matter of fact, Diamond wasn't sure if she ever wanted to see Shymeek's face again. Every time she thought about what she caught him and D-Nice doing in their bed, it made her sick. Diamond picked up the phone to call Brooklyn's house to see if Brooklyn's aunt had a number where she could reach Brooklyn right now. When Brooklyn answered the phone, Diamond started crying as soon as she recognized Brooklyn's voice.

"Diamond?!? What's wrong? Why are you crying?" Brooklyn asked concerned.

"Brooklyn, I caught that bitch mutha fucka in the bed with D-Nice."

"What? You caught Shymeek and D-Nice in the bed with somebody?" Brooklyn hadn't caught on yet.

"NO! I caught him and D-Nice in the bed. He was fucking D-Nice!" Diamond said sternly.

"What?!!! Girl, where are you?" Brooklyn was still a little

bit confused. The shit she just heard sounded crazy.

"I'm at a hotel in New Jersey."

"What the hell are you doing in New Jersey?" Brooklyn walked into the kitchen and looked in the refrigerator.

"I was just driving, trying to clear my head. I didn't have anyplace else to go. I just found myself driving and ended up here."

"When did this happen?" Brooklyn was sipping on some Kool-Aid.

"I caught the mutha fucka last night."

"Diamond, come to my house. I'll be here waiting for you. Aight? Hurry up."

"Aight. Peace!" Diamond hung up the phone.

• • •

After Rahmel and China left the storefront, they went to China's house. China sat on the couch with her legs spread while Rahmel sniffed cocaine and ate China's pussy at the same time. They were celebrating their latest victory. The last couple of weeks, China had been sniffing more coke than she did her entire life and she had been sniffing since she was sixteen. She and Rahmel had been cramming that shit up their noses like it was going out of style. It was as if Rahmel needed cocaine to stimulate his sex drive. They sniffed over an ounce a day. Between each sniff of coke, Rahmel licked and sucked China's clit. China's vagina was numb from the cocaine that was on Rahmel's face and tongue as he ate her out. Not to mention that China was too high herself to accurately respond to Rahmel's pussy eating ability. They had been getting high since they came back into the house. Alfonso stashed the drugs they took from Divine, but Rahmel took two keys for his own personal use. China sniffed line after line up her nose as she squirmed her hips while Rahmel handled his business with his mouth. China had just finished giving Rahmel the monster leg shaking, meanest, dick suck too. They were both on cloud nine enhanced by the cocaine when the doorbell rang.

"Oh, shit, Daddy, hold up. That's the doorbell." China fiddled with her nose.

"Don't answer it," Rahmel said. His eyes were wide and his nose was red like Rudolf the reindeer.

"I have to. I forgot that April was supposed to come by tonight and do my hair. Baby, hold up. I'll get rid of her quick," China said as she got up, closed her robe, wiped the residue off of her face and went to answer the door. Rahmel sat on the couch and continued sniffing the cocaine they had on the table.

April was a shorty from around the way that was one of the best hair stylists in Bedstuy. She was known for her skills and her name had a buzz in the hood for doing everybody's hair. April was only sixteen and too young to work in anybody's beauty salon, so she made house calls. April made a good living off of doing hair. She charged from 100 to 150 a head, and her customers had no problem giving her the money because she was the best. Everybody that was somebody came to her to get their hair done, and if you didn't have an appointment with her but needed your hair done in an emergency, of course that would cost you an extra fifty dollars. Most of April's people were all of the hustlers' girls. She was responsible for all of their styles, even Brooklyn's.

As soon as China opened the door and let April in, the first thing she noticed was Rahmel sitting in front of a pile of cocaine on the coffee table. Just earlier, April heard of the war between Divine and Rahmel. April was fucking lil Remo and was with him when the fiend came and told Remo what happened to Kyzm, Black and Soldier. And she knew that the word on the streets was that Rahmel was responsible. April also knew that at one time Divine used to fuck with China and now China had the nigga that Divine had beef with up in her crib damn near naked getting coked out of his mind. April looked into China's glassy eyes and knew she was high out of her mind. Something wasn't right with this picture.

"What's up, girl? Are you ready to get your hair done?" April asked. She hoped that China would reschedule their appointment.

"What's up, April? Girl, I forgot all about our appointment tonight. It's not a good time right now because I have company. Can I reschedule for tomorrow night?"

"Girl, you know that my weekends are all booked up. I'm backed up until next week."

"Damn, well I apologize. I'ma have to see you next week, okay?" China said as she escorted April to the door, damn near pushing her out.

As soon as April left China's house, she pulled out her cell phone and paged lil Remo.

Chapter 15
Under Miami's Moon

Raul's people told Divine that the van would be parked out front with the keys in it. As lil Remo pulled up in front of the warehouse on Rockaway and 145th, they spotted the van.

"These niggas just left two hundred keys right under everybody's nose and no one would ever suspect it," Divine said as he jumped out of Whop's truck. "Yo, Remo, y'all go to the crib and get Kali and Biheem and meet me back at the warehouse on Lex."

Whop jumped out the truck, left Remo, ran over and got in the van with Divine.

"Yo, Vine, I'ma ride with you, ya heard?" Whop said.

"Aight, let's go, baby. U-N-I," Divine said as he pulled off in the van.

Lil Remo pulled off behind them, but instead of making a left on the VanWick going towards Brooklyn, he made a right going deeper into Queens. As Remo drove vibing to Jay-Z's *Black album*, his pager went off. It was April's cell phone number followed by 911. Remo and April had been fucking around since they were both in summer school last year. Remo was only a year older than she was. They had recently broken up, but they were still fucking each other. So Remo immediately called April back.

"Yo, what's up, boo?" Remo said, trying to sound sexy.

"Remo, I just left that bitch China's house and guess who was there getting coked up with her?"

"Who? We have been trying to reach that bitch since yesterday." He was on point now.

"She had that cat Rahmel there. They just finished fucking. He had a pile of cocaine on the table in front of him snorting his brains out and that bitch was there sucking that nigga dry. He's laid up in her house like he lives there."

"Word! That bitch! I knew that bitch had something to do with all this shit going on. Yo, April, I'ma call you back tonight. I have to call Divine. Thanks for letting me know that." As soon as Remo hung up the phone from April, he dialed Divine's cell phone.

• • •

Angel had signed herself out of the hospital. The monkey was on her back and she was fiending to smoke some crack. That shit had been calling her since she came out of the coma. She tried her best to fight the urge, but it got the best of her. Angel felt bad because she had made Diamond a promise that she was about to break. It wasn't her fault—she was an addict and the drug was stronger than she was. Rahmel had broken her spirit and her strength. The first thing Angel did when she left the hospital was go straight to a pawnshop where she pawned the diamond ring that Diamond had given her. She figured that she would pawn it instead of selling it so that she would be able to go back and get it. The man in the pawnshop gave Angel four hundred dollars for the ring. Angel ran to the first crack house that she found. As she took that first hit, tears started to fall and she succumbed to her demons. With each hit she took, she would cry more and more. She was too far gone. Angel loved her daughter, but that crack shit had her...

• • •

When Diamond reached Brooklyn's house and Brooklyn opened the door, she hugged Brooklyn and started crying. Diamond told Brooklyn everything that had happened over again. Diamond and Brooklyn spent that night getting drunk while Diamond vented everything that she was going through. Brooklyn just let her friend vent because she knew it wasn't too much that she could say or do to comfort her best friend, so she was just there to lend a faithful heart, silent tongue and a listening ear. Brooklyn loved Diamond just as much as she loved any of her family, maybe even a little more. She wished that it was something that she could do or say that would ease Diamond's pain. They both had it rough growing up, but Diamond always had it a little worse. When Shymeek first came into Diamond's life and brought a smile on her friend's face, Brooklyn was happy for Diamond. Now the same nigga was responsible for destroying her emotionally.

"Listen, Diamond, Divine has a couple of houses that he doesn't use. I know he wouldn't mind renting one of them out to you and Angel. He knows about y'all's situation, so I'm sure he won't stress y'all about the rent."

"Brooklyn, I appreciate everything you and Divine have done for me and my mother. The rent wouldn't be a problem. I have a couple of g's in the bank. As a matter of fact, I have a joint bank account with that nigga. I got to get up early in the morning and empty that shit out."

"Diamond, what are you going to do about Shymeek and

the baby?"

Diamond wasn't expecting that one. "I'm keeping my baby, but as far as Shymeek goes, fuck him. He would never see me or my baby ever again. How would I be able to explain to my son that his father sleeps with men? That mutha fucka will never lay eyes on my child." Diamond rolled her eyes.

"What are you going to do about his Range Rover?"

"Fuck his truck. I should burn that mutha fucka," Diamond said as she guzzled down the last little bit of Blue Alize she had in her glass.

As Diamond sat, drowning out her misery, her cell phone went off. Diamond looked at the caller I.D. that the cell phone had and it showed a number Diamond didn't recognize, so she answered it.

"Who is it?" she screamed into the phone.

"Diamond, please, don't hang up. Let me explain. I need to tal..."

Before Shymeek could finish what he was saying, Diamond hung up the phone. "I wish that bitch ass nigga would stop calling me. He need to be worrying about that nigga D-Nice. He wasn't worrying about me when he had his dick all up in that nigga's ass," Diamond said as she turned off her cell phone.

Diamond and Brooklyn drank and smoked weed until they both crashed out on the living room floor.

Early the next morning, Diamond and Brooklyn went to the bank and Diamond took all the money that she and Shymeek had in a joint account and closed the account. Then she and Brooklyn went to Juniors for lunch. While they ate their lunch, Diamond's doctor called her on her cell phone and told her that all the results from her test and cultures came back and that she needed to come in and speak with him as soon as possible. Diamond started to worry. "What is so important that he wants me to come in as soon as possible. Why couldn't he tell me what he had to tell me over the phone?" Diamond asked Brooklyn.

Diamond started to get nervous. *Is something wrong with me or the baby?* Diamond questioned herself.

After they finished their lunch, Diamond and Brooklyn went back to Brooklyn's house to put up the money and then went to the doctor's office.

• • •

Shymeek stayed up all night trying to reach Diamond. He knew the only place she had to go was to Brooklyn's house and Shymeek knew better than to go there looking for her. Because he knew Brooklyn's man was a killer and he didn't want any problems with him or his crew. D-Nice had gone back to Atlanta. He wasn't trying to get all involved or caught up in Shymeek's mess. He had to handle Diamond on his own. D-Nice told Shymeek that he should have told Diamond that he was a homo. Now that the cat was out of the bag, Shymeek had to handle it on his own. D-Nice was comfortable with his sexuality; he had nothing to hide. When D-Nice left, he told Shymeek that he would see him when he came to Atlanta the following week for their studio session.

That morning, Shymeek went to the bank to try and take out his share of his and Diamond's joint account. The bank teller told him that a young lady by the name of Diamond Weatherspoon had come by earlier and took out all the money and closed the account. Shymeek couldn't believe it. Diamond had taken over forty thousand of his money. "Damn! I knew I should have come here earlier. That stinking bitch! I'll fix her broke ass," Shymeek said as he walked out of the bank.

As soon as Shymeek got in the house, he called the police

and reported his truck stolen.

• • •

When Divine and the crew finished unloading half of the cocaine off of the van into the warehouse, King Jolly was to take the other half to the Bronx. King Jolly ran all Divine's drug operations in the Bronx. He was Divine's partner that ran the Bronx. Jolly had a stronghold in the Bronx. He had at least thirty runners or better. Divine had met Jolly through his brother Wonderful. Jolly was one of the original Latin Kings from the Bronx. He first met Wonderful and Draz on the *Island* back in '87 when he first started his fifteen-year bid. Jolly and Wonderful were the reason that the five percent and the Latin Kings squashed their beef. The Kings had paid Wonderful and Draz to put some work in on some cats that tapped one of their stashes of dope they had and that the dude was heavy into the black power movement, so it would have caused a war if one of the other races moved on him. Wonderful and Draz weren't feeling that the nigga was on some sneak thief time. So they took it as an opportunity. The Kings controlled the dope in C74. Wonderful knew that the Kings couldn't allow that to happen without losing face. He also knew that they didn't want to risk a full out war with the blacks. So Wonderful and Draz stepped to Jolly with a proposition. The proposition was that if they hit the cat that tapped their stash that Jolly and the Kings would cut the Gods in. That was the beginning of their relationship. Wonderful was murdered before Jolly came home. Jolly stayed in contact with Divine. Divine was the one sending shorties to visit them with tons of shit stuffed in their pussies. When Jolly came home, Divine blessed Jolly with two keys. That was supposed to be their come up in the Bronx, but Divine got locked up. Jolly kept to his word and when Divine came home, Jolly signed Divine's name to the deed of an apartment building that he had bought with the money he made off the work that Divine had originally given him. But when Divine came home he was ready to take it to another level. He had the Columbians backing him and he had a mean team with him ready to get that money. So it was only right that he reunited with his man and get that Bronx money as well. Divine gave Jolly twenty-five keys from the gate and he and his crew of s1's proceeded to lock the Bronx down. Jolly and all of his workers lived by a code. *If you fuck with our money, death was the penalty.* And they meant it.

Jolly and his Kings planted fear in the hearts of the Bronx. That was why he was given the title of King. Divine gave Jolly the hundred keys for nine thousand a piece which would have brought back $900,000. Divine would give fifty to Mo'Better and the other fifty he would give to his crew to move out of the spots in Brooklyn. This was how he would make a profit. Right now it was time for war. Divine had to focus on what he was doing because already seven of his people had been murdered by some fake ass niggas. When Jolly departed, he left is lil gunman, King Gangsta, as an extra gun for Divine.

Remo told Divine what April had told him about the bitch China and Rahmel. As Remo was explaining everything that April had told him, Divine's pager went off. Divine called the number back and it was Killa's shorty from the projects. She told him that Killa and Draz were murdered in a hotel room and that the homicide police had just left the crib showing them pictures of Draz and Killa's bodies filled with holes. She told Divine that she and Killa's mother just came back from identifying the body. Divine *now* knew for sure that China was behind everything.

"Yo, son, that was Ronda, Killa and Draz were found dead

in a hotel room," Divine said to Remo.

"What?"

"Ronda said that she and Killa's mother just came back from identifying his body." Divine balled up his fist and mouthed the words, "I'ma kill that bitch *and* that bitch ass nigga."

"Yo, they were supposed to meet up with that bitch China to set up that nigga Rahmel at a hotel."

"Yo, come on yo, let's go. We're gonna get that bitch *and* him tonight," Divine said.

• • •

After hours of fucking, sucking and snorting, China was out like a light. She was laid across the bed naked with her ass up in the air, sore, with her legs spread. Rahmel had fucked her every which way that was possible. Rahmel got dressed and left. He had to meet up with Alfonso. They planned on hitting Divine's spot on Jefferson and Broadway that evening. Rahmel was enjoying the cat and mouse game he and Divine were playing. To Rahmel, Divine and his crew were a bunch of young boys making a lot of money. Rahmel jumped into his hooptie and pulled off.

Chapter 16
Life's A Bitch, Then You Die

When the nurse at the desk called Diamond's name and told her that the doctor would see her, knots started to form in her stomach. Diamond told Brooklyn to hold her bags as she got up and went to the back towards the doctor's office. Diamond never liked going to see the doctor. Even as a child she dreaded the doctor's office and hospitals. They always gave her the feeling of death. The phobia in her still existed. As she walked into the office, the doctor was at his desk looking through a file he had in front of him. When Diamond walked in, the doctor looked up.

"Oh, yes, how are you feeling today, Ms. Weatherspoon?" The doctor greeted Diamond with a smile.

"I'm alright, just a little tired." Diamond was nervous.

"Have a seat, please. The reason I called you in here today is because the results to all the blood work we did on you, which is our normal procedure for all our expecting mothers, one of the things we check your blood work for is any viruses or diseases, mainly HIV. And the test shows that your blood has been infected with the HIV virus."

Diamond dropped her head into her hands and started

crying.

"Ms. Weatherspoon, this doesn't mean that your life is over. Many people are still living full lives with the virus. As long as you take the medication and take good care of yourself, you can still live a full life."

Diamond couldn't believe what had just been told to her. Everything was as if it was moving in slow motion. The only person that she had ever had unprotected sex with was Shymeek. *That bitch, faggot mutha fucka gave me this shit,"* Diamond thought to herself as the doctor spoke to her. After the words *"your blood has been infected with the HIV virus,"* Diamond no longer heard anything that the doctor was saying to her. Her life was destroyed and Shymeek was the blame.

"What about my baby?" Diamond asked as she tried to regain her composure.

"We really can't tell right now if the baby has been exposed to the virus, Ms. Weatherspoon. I want you to contact this number. This is a crisis center for young mothers living with the HIV and AIDS virus," the doctor said as he wrote down the number and gave it to Diamond. "I'm also prescribing you some medication to see how your body responds to it. The baby won't be affected by the medication. Ms. Weatherspoon, it's very important that you contact the people at the crisis center. They can help you cope. There are plenty of young women your age that are going through the same thing that you are. You don't have to do this alone. Remember, you can still live a full life. This doesn't mean that your life is over. I'm setting you up for another appointment in two weeks."

Diamond got up, shook the doctor's hand and left the office. Diamond tried to get herself together before she got to where Brooklyn was seated waiting for her. As soon as Diamond walked over to Brooklyn, Brooklyn took one look at her best friend and knew something was wrong and that Diamond had been crying.

"Diamond, what's wrong?" Brooklyn asked. Brooklyn looked as if she wanted to cry herself.

Diamond dropped her head down and started crying hysterically. She couldn't help it. Brooklyn jumped up and hugged her.

"Diamond, what happened? What's wrong?" Brooklyn caressed her friend's back.

"Brooklyn, that nigga gave me *that shit*," Diamond said over her tears.

"What shit?" Brooklyn backed up off of her friend and took a look at her.

"The monster! HIV!" Diamond yelled.

"Oh, God! No!" Brooklyn said as she hugged Diamond tighter and started crying.

Diamond and Brooklyn left the doctor's office both in tears. Brooklyn drove while Diamond sat in silence thinking how her life had changed so drastically and fast. Diamond thought about dying and how she hoped that her child wasn't affected by the virus. Diamond said a silent prayer for her unborn child.

"Brooklyn, take me to see my mother. I need to see my mother."

"Diamond, how are you holding up over there?" Brooklyn looked over at her troubled home girl.

"I can't believe how this nigga fucked up my life." Diamond wiped her tears and stared out the window as Brooklyn cruised down the street.

When they arrived at the hospital, the nurse told Diamond that Angel had signed herself out of the hospital against the wishes of her doctors. Diamond couldn't believe that Angel just up and left. "Where could she have gone? Angel didn't know where Shymeek lived, so she couldn't have gone to his house" Diamond said to Brooklyn as they jumped into Shymeek's truck and pulled off. Diamond called over to Mrs. Sheena's house to see if her mother had gone over there or if she was next door. Mrs. Sheena told Diamond that Angel hadn't come by her apartment but to hold on while she checked to see if she was next door. When Mrs. Sheena returned to the phone, she told Diamond that nobody was across the hall and that if Angel stopped by that she would call her. After Diamond hung up the phone with Mrs. Sheena, Brooklyn told her to call her house to see if Angel went over there. Brooklyn's aunt told Diamond that Angel hadn't stopped by there yet either. But if she did, she would let her know that Diamond was looking for her.

"Diamond, do you think that Angel would have hooked back up with your father?" Brooklyn asked.

"Nah, I don't think my moms would ever do that," Diamond responded. Diamond never told Brooklyn about Angel's addiction. So that could have been a possibility but she prayed to God that it wasn't the case.

"Does your father still live in the same place that y'all used to live at?"

"Yeah, that mutha fucka still lives there." Diamond rolled her eyes.

Brooklyn made a mental note to herself to be sure to let Divine know that little bit of information. As they pulled up to the light on the corner of Atlantic and Utica, a police car pulled up behind them and flashed their lights.

WHOOP! WHOOP! WHOOP!

• • •

Once everybody reached the house in Queens, Divine started putting their moves into effect.

"Yo, Kali, I want you to take Byheem and Gangsta with you to that bitch China's house. If nobody is there, wait for them to show. We got to kill that bitch tonight. Hold up, as a matter of fact, Remo, I need you to go with them to handle this, just in case that nigga Rahmel shows up. And you know what the nigga look like and you now where the bitch lives."

Kali, lil Remo, Gangsta and Byheem left the crib and they all jumped into the hooptie war wagon that Byheem was driving.

"Yo, Whop, I need you and I-Shine to travel with me. We're going to hit up that nigga Alfonso. I found out that he owns a house in Lower Manhattan. He lives there with his wife and a newborn baby," Divine requested.

"Yo, son, how in the hell you find all that shit out about that nigga?" Whop asked.

"I had my man Mo'Better have one of his baby's mothers that work in DMV run the plates from that nigga's car for me and she gave the nigga's whole rundown. The car was registered in his wife's name. So we're going to move on this nigga around four in the morning. That way we can catch the nigga in bed or I hope he's up fucking so we can fuck up his nut. Ya heard?" Divine smiled.

"Yo, Vine, have you heard anything from Kyzm, Black or Soldier's family yet?"

"I haven't spoken to anybody yet because I've been on the move since I got back from Miami."

"Divine, how was them niggas able to get out on y'all like that, son?" I-Shine asked as he lit the blunt he had rolled.

"Yo, God, I used to fuck with that cat. We used to sell this nigga bricks of that thing. I never trusted that nigga as far as I could throw him. He's one of them old time shady niggas. Once Meth and 'em told me that they saw the nigga fucking with the Panamanians from up the block, I knew I had to watch the nigga. I sent that chick, China, that we used to set niggas up for us to get close to them and find out what they was up to. You know we used China for that type of work plenty of times and not to mention that I used to fuck the bitch. As a matter of fact, I fucked the bitch right before I sent her at Rahmel. I fucked that bitch against my own will. I ran into her at the Apollo when I was with Brooklyn. When I told her I was there with my girl, the bitch caught a little attitude. She act like she was fiending for a nigga to hit that. So when that shit went down with the niggas hitting up the block and Meth and Tank getting killed, I needed her, so I had to sling the dick to the bitch. Somehow that nigga Rahmel flipped her," Divine explained.

"Yo, God, you know it's hard to get money *and* war. So the money has to be put on hold until we get these niggas."

"Yeah, I know son. I already shut down all the operations in Brooklyn. Jolly still got the Bronx pumping and Mo'Better still doing his thing in Harlem. And between the both of them handling their business, the money should still flow smoothly. Our main focus right now is getting at them Panamanians and Rahmel," Divine concluded.

"Yeah, let's do it," Whop said.

• • •

China lived on the first floor of a brownstone house in Bushwick. When Byheem pulled on her block, Remo told him to park the car closer to the corner as they got out and walked up on foot to China's house. It was 2 a.m. in the morning and the block was empty.

"Yo, this is her crib right here," Remo said in a whisper.
China's building had bars on the first and second floor windows.

"Yo, son, how the fuck are we getting up in this mutha fucka? It's caged up like a fortress," Byheem asked.

"Come on," Remo said as he walked in front of China's gate.

"Yo, Remo, what's up," Byheem questioned.

"We're going around the block so we can get in through the back yard," Remo answered.

"How?"

"We're gonna have to cut through a vacant lot."

They all walked around the block in a fast pace and they had to climb over a fence to get to China's backyard. China's back windows had bars on them as well. Kali checked the back door and it was locked.

"Yo, it don't look like anyone is home," Gangsta said as he looked through the window.

"Yeah, but be on point anyway," Byheem said as he pulled out his gat.

Everybody followed suit and they all pulled out their guns. Kali walked up to the back door and gave it a little shove with his shoulder and saw that if he gave it a harder shove that the door would give way. "Yo, I can push this shit open."

"Word! Let's do it."

"Yo, is everybody ready?" Kali asked. At the same time he gave the door another shove and the door flew open. They all ran into the house with their guns out.

They each ran into a separate room. The first two rooms and the kitchen were empty. When Remo and Kali walked into the bedroom, China was laying across her bed naked fast asleep. Gangsta and Byheem held the front door down while

Kali and Remo walked into China's room and stood over her. She was out. Remo's dick got hard as he looked at China's naked body. Remo had always wanted to hit it but at the time, she was fucking with Divine. He thought about hitting it now before they murdered the bitch. Remo hated to see some good pussy go to waste. Kali walked up to China and smacked her across the face with the butt of his gun.

CRACK!!!

You could hear the bones break in her face. China jumped up grabbing her face in pain. Kali threw his gun in her face.

"Bitch, you set up my mans and them and thought you were going to get away with it, huh? You didn't think we were gonna find out? Where's that nigga Rahmel at? As a matter of fact, bitch, don't answer that. We'll find that mutha fucka on our own," Kali said as he raised his pistol to China's head and pulled the trigger.

POP...POP, POP, POP!!!

China's body slumped over the edge of the bed and they all ran out the back door, the same way they came in.

Chapter 17

When It Rains, It Pours

The police approached the Range Rover with their guns out.

"Turn the engine off, now!" one of the officers yelled.

"Driver, place both hands out of the window," the assisting officer demanded.

As the police snatched both women out of the car, Brooklyn tried to ask the police what the problem was. But the police ignored her and threw them both to the ground. Diamond screamed that she was pregnant as she was thrown to the ground and the handcuffs placed on her. Once they both were handcuffed and put into the squad cars, they were told that the truck they were driving was reported stolen. They were both arrested and taken to jail.

When they went in front of the judge the next morning, they were both R.O.R.'d (released on their own recognizance) and given another court date to appear before the judge. All night Brooklyn tried to get in contact with Divine, but he wasn't answering his cell phone. They were lucky that they had a C.O. that allowed her to keep trying. The fact that the C.O. was feeling Brooklyn helped out a lot.

As soon as they left the courthouse, Diamond decided to call Shymeek. Shymeek answered his phone on the first ring.

"Yo," he said.

"Why did you tell the police that your truck was stolen? Do you know that me and Brooklyn just got out of jail?" Diamond said angrily.

"You and that bitch had no business in my mutha fucking truck. Why did you take my shit? Bitch, you stole my shit. And what's up with my fucking money, bitch?"

"Oh, now I'm a bitch? Nigga, you ain't shit. Do you know that your nasty ass gave me that shit? Yeah, nigga, we're both gonna die but you're gonna die first. You going to get yours, nigga, believe that. You will answer for this shit you did to my life. You bitch faggot, mutha fucka," Diamond said before she hung up the phone on Shymeek.

While Brooklyn spoke on the phone with her aunt, Diamond waved down a cab.

• • •

After Rahmel left China's house, he went to pick up Mike Dred and Red. Mike Dred and Red were two dope fiend brothers that Rahmel used to put in work for him. Mike and Red were the ones who murdered Kyzm and who hit Draz and Killa in the hotel. Rahmel grew up under them. The brothers were a couple of years older than Rahmel. They all grew up in Brooklyn. Mike and Red at one time were two of the biggest heroin dealers in Brooklyn in the late 70s and early 80s. They both caught a twenty-year bid in '85 for murder. During their bid they both started using heroin heavy to cope with the twenty years they had to do. By the time they both came home in 2002, they had a mean habit. Rahmel knew their potential and he knew that the brothers were cold blooded killers, so as soon as they came home, Rahmel snatched them up, gave them money and a place to live and they have been putting in work for him ever since. Rahmel paid them a good amount of money but every dime he gave them went into their arms. Rahmel rented them a basement apartment in a house he owned in Crown Heights. After Rahmel picked the brothers up, he drove to meet up with Alfonso. Alfonso told Rahmel that he would give him two hundred fifty thousand for his share of the cocaine that they took from Divine. Since it was Alfonso who got the police car and it was his people who posed as the cops and murdered Black and Soldier, Alfonso felt Rahmel would be happy with two hundred fifty g's. Rahmel agreed to Alfonso's offer. *Fuck it, it was guaranteed cash. Rahmel wasn't guaranteed that he would be able to sell a hundred keys. Anything could happen.* So he figured the money would be better even though he knew if he sold the coke, he could make over a million dollars. He would give Mike, Red and China ten a piece, or give Mike and Red five a piece and give China ten and still have two hundred thirty for himself. Rahmel considered himself the one coming out on top, not to mention, once he got rid of these lil niggas on the block, he would have the building and would make a killing anyway. After Rahmel got his money from Alfonso, he dropped the money off and then he and his two dope fiend killers went looking for trouble. They drove by Divine's spot on Jefferson and Broadway, but the gate was down. They drove through the block of the building and it was like a ghost town.

"Fuck it, them niggas are somewhere hiding. I told you them niggas were just lil boys," Rahmel said as he sniffed some coke he had in a one hundred dollar bill as Mike drove. "Yo, Mike, drive me to my little bitch house. I need my head polished."

As soon as they entered China's block, they spotted police activity in front of China's crib and the front of the building taped off as if it were a crime scene. Mike pulled over and asked one of China's neighbors what was going on. He told Mike that a girl named China had been murdered. Rahmel felt a sharp pain in his stomach when China's name came out of the man's mouth. But Rahmel quickly chalked it up. Better her than him, was how he felt. That just meant that he had to hurry up and kill Divine before Divine killed him.

"Yo, let's go." As Mike pulled off, Rahmel said, "That was a waste of some good pussy." He sniffed his cocaine and laid back.

• • •

Divine, Whop and I-Shine pulled up on Alfonso's block. Alfonso lived in a two-family house in the middle of the block.

"Yo, I, stay in the car while Whop and I go inside. Keep the car running. We're gonna go in there handle this mutha fucka and get the fuck out of there. Yo, Whop, do you have all of your tools?" Divine asked.

"Yeah, let's do this."

Back in the days growing up, Whop was called the locksmith because there wasn't a house or car that Whop couldn't break into. With a bobby pin and a nail file, Whop could pick any lock. As soon as Whop got out the car, he had Alfonso's door open within three minutes. Divine and Whop entered the house. The first room they peeped in had all type of baby shit in it. It had a crib and stuffed animals all over it. This had to be the newborn's room. In the second room, they noticed two adult bodies lying up under the sheets. Divine and Whop tiptoed into the room and stood over the bed. It was as if Alfonso felt their presence because as soon as Divine stood over him,

Alfonso opened his eyes. Alfonso noticed shadows standing over him and sat up. At the same time, Divine pointed a big ass 44 Desert Eagle at his head. Alfonso froze at the sight of the big ass nozzle of the gun pointed at his face. Alfonso's wife turned over and said something to him in Spanish. Slowly she opened her eyes and noticed two figures standing over them pointing guns at them. She started screaming.

"Aaaahh!"

"Shut up, bitch," Divine yelled at the broad.

CRACK!!

Whop smacked Alfonso's wife in the face with the butt of his gun. She grabbed her face while blood shot out from her mouth and nose.

"What's up, Alfonso? Where is my coke?" Divine said. He turned on the lamp that was on the nightstand with his free hand while he kept his gun pointed at Alfonso's head. He wanted Alfonso to see his face.

"What coke? Who are you? What do y'all want?" Alfonso questioned. He was still half asleep and confused.

"Oh, you don't know what coke I'm talking about, huh? And you don't know who I am? Okay! Whop."

Whop raised his gun and fired.

BUNG! BUNG, BUNG!!

"Noooo!!" Alfonso screamed as he watched his wife of ten years' body slump over on the bed.

"Now, Alfonso, do you want your newborn baby in the other room to meet the same fate as your lovely wife did? I don't think so. Now I'm going to ask you one more time. Where is my cocaine at?" Divine asked again.

"Please, don't kill my baby," Alfonso said as he grabbed his wife's corpse. He was crying like a baby.

"Answer my question. Where is my coke?" Divine pointed

his hammer at Alfonso's head.

"It's stashed in a van I have parked in one of my car lots."

"Where is this lot of yours?" Divine mushed Alfonso hard with the tip of the Desert.

"It's on Atlantic and Franklin. The keys to the lot are on the dresser with the keys to the van."

"Keep an eye on him," Divine told Whop while he went to the dresser.

Divine pulled out two sets of keys and a stack of hundreds held together with rubber bands.

"These?" Divine asked as he held up the two sets of keys that were on a loop.

"Yes," Alfonso said in a faint voice.

"Thank you."

BUNG, BUNG, BUNG, BUNG, BUNG!!!

Divine hit Alfonso in the face and head with five shots. Then Divine threw the money he took off the dresser to Whop. They walked out the house and as they got into the car, Divine told I-Shine to drive to Atlantic and Franklin. Whop counted up twenty-five thousand dollars. Divine told him that they would give that to help out with the funerals.

Twenty minutes later, they pulled up to the corner of Atlantic and Franklin and on the right hand side there was the car lot. The lot was filled with all of the newest cars and in the back of the lot a brown colored van stood out. They all jumped out of the car when Divine opened the gate. The group entered the premises and Divine opened the back of the van and there was his coke. Divine looked at Whop and I-Shine and they all smiled. Divine jumped in the van, started it up and pulled out of the lot. Whop and I-Shine jumped back in the car they came in and pulled off behind Divine.

• • •

As Rahmel, Mike and Red were driving back from China's house, Rahmel spotted someone he thought he recognized. He could have sworn that the woman he saw walking the streets like she was tricking was Angel from a distance. As they got closer, he realized that it was Angel. She looked like she was strung out, way out there. She had lost all of her weight and looked like death. Rahmel couldn't believe it. This couldn't be his Angel. Rahmel told Mike to pull up beside the lady walking. Red asked Rahmel if he was trying to get some head from this crackhead bitch? As they pulled up beside her, Angel bent down into the car's window and asked them did they want to party and that she would fuck and suck all of their dicks for fifty dollars. Rahmel was shocked that this was his one-time beautiful wife and the mother of his daughter. Tears started forming in the corner of his eyes. Rahmel still had love for Angel and it hurt him to see her like this. *She's too far gone. She doesn't even recognize me,* Rahmel thought to himself. "Angel, what happened to you?"

Angel looked into the back seat when she heard the person in the back say her name. That's when she realized to whom she was talking. Mike and Red both looked at Rahmel with a puzzled look on their faces.

"You did this to me," Angel said as she walked away from the car and started running. Rahmel sat in silence as tears started falling down his face. He realized how much he really cared about Angel.

Chapter 18

It's Going Down

As Kali pulled up to the light on the corner of Dekalb and Malcolm X, a police car pulled up beside them and looked into the car. Everybody tried not to look suspicious, but the fact that they were four deep in a car and everybody had on hoodies in seventy-five degree weather didn't help any. As the light turned green, Kali pulled off. Kali looked through the rearview mirror and realized that the police were following them. After they followed them for a couple of blocks without turning off, everybody started to panic.

"Yo, don't nobody turn around, just be cool," Kali said nervously.

"Son, we have a car full of heat, not to mention the smoking gun that we just murdered a mutha fucka with. If these pigs try to pull us over, we're going down. And I'm not trying to go out like that. I'ma hold court in the streets," Gangsta said as he pulled out his heat.

"Everybody just stay cool," Byheem said as he turned around to see if the police were still behind them. "Maybe they're just trying to make us panic so we can do something stupid or reckless. Just drive careful."

"Yo, fuck that son, if they act crazy and pull us over, we're gonna light their asses up," Remo said as he cocked the pin on the mac he had.

As Kali turned onto Dekalb and Marcy, the police flashed their lights.

"Yo, they're pulling us over."

"Kali, breeze on them mutha fuckas," Byheem said as he turned around in his seat measuring the distance between them and the police.

"Nah, Blood, this piece of shit will never outrun them. I'ma pull over and as soon as they get out their car to approach us, we jump out and start dumping at them. Ya heard?"

"Aight, let's do it," Remo said as he held up his heat to show that he was ready.

WHOOP! WHOOP! WHOOP!

As Kali pulled over, the police got out their squad car and started walking toward the foursome. All four doors of the hooptie swung open. Kali, Remo, Gangsta and Byheem all jumped out firing at the police.

BLATTA! BLATTA!...BOOM, BOOM! POP, POP, POP, POP! BOOM! BOOM! BLATTA! BLATTA!!

Both officers dove for cover behind the patrol car's doors as slugs tore through the hood, doors and the windshield.

"I'm hit," one of the officers screamed as he fell to the ground grabbing the side of his face in pain.

The rookie officer took aim from behind the car door and returned fire.

BUNG, BUNG, BUNG, BUNG, BUNG, BUNG, BUNG, BUNG!!!

Byheem went down as Kali, Gangsta and Remo continued to knock at the police car. Gangsta ran toward the police car firing. He was determined to kill some police.

POP, POP, POP, POP, POP, POP, POP!!!
BUNG, BUNG, BUNG, BUNG, BUNG, BUNG!!!
The rookie officer returned shots firing frantically as he watched Gangsta's slugs pierce his partner's skull. His body pulsated viciously on the ground next to the squad car. Gangsta went down as blood poured from his head. Kali and Remo kept firing as they ran and jumped into their hooptie and sped off. The rookie officer radioed in. "Shots fired. Officer down."

"Yo, Blood, you aight?" Kali looked to his man to see if he was hit.

"Yeah, son, I'm aight. You?" Remo asked as he popped in another clip in his gat.

"Yo, Blood, we got to ditch this ride. This shit is hot right about now," Kali suggested.

After they felt like they were far enough, Kali pulled over and they jumped out of the hooptie. Remo hit the window of a Nissan Sentra that was parked in front of them.

"Come on, son, let's go," Remo said as he hotwired the car.

● ● ●

As Rahmel sat at his table sniffing the raw, he couldn't get Angel out of his mind. Rahmel couldn't believe Angel was fucked up like that. Rahmel looked at Mike and Red who were both in a dope fiend nod.

"Yo, ya'll had no idea who that was, do y'all?" Rahmel asked his intoxicated partners.

"Nah, why you still stressing that crackhead bitch, youngin'? We can go to any corner and get one of them bitches to suck your head for you, if that's what you want," Red said as he drifted back into one of his dope nods.

"Nah, it ain't that, old timer. It's bigger than that. That was my wife and the mother of my oldest daughter. That was

Angel. At one time she was the baddest bitch in Brooklyn. I hadn't seen her in three years, and to see her like that did something to me," Rahmel said as he took another line up his nose.

"Word, youngin', that was that lil pretty thing I used to see you with before we got locked up?" Mike asked.

"Yeah, Mike, that was my Angel. Yo, come on, y'all, let's go," Rahmel said as he threw the car keys to Red. "I have to go get her. She needs me," Rahmel said and they walked out the door.

• • •

When Diamond and Brooklyn reached Brooklyn's house, Diamond headed straight for Brooklyn's bed. For the rest of that day and night, Diamond didn't get out of the bed. Brooklyn tried her best to comfort her friend, but Diamond wasn't in the mood for anything. She was depressed, full of self-pity and afraid. All she could think about was death and the images of Shymeek's cock in D-Nice's ass. After hours of stressing and crying, Diamond finally fell off to sleep. Brooklyn had finally reached Divine a little after one in the morning.

"Divine, I have been trying to reach you for two days. Do you have any idea what I've been through?" Brooklyn spoke serenely, but she was still a little upset.

"Brooklyn, you know that I've been going through it lately. I'm not trying to duck you. I just don't want you getting caught up in any of this shit with that nigga Rahmel."

"Divine, I'ma rider. I'm ready to ride for you. Let me be the one that holds you down."

"Yeah, boo, you know I like to hear you talk like that, but I have niggas around me for that."

"Daddy, fuck them. They won't give their life for you like I'm willing to do."

"Don't worry about it, boo. Everything is gonna be alright. I have family around me."

"Daddy, me and Diamond just got out of jail."

"What?! Out of jail? For what?"

"That nigga Shymeek told the police that his car was stolen. That nigga had the nerve to say that we carjacked him." Divine started laughing.

"Daddy, don't laugh. It's some serious shit going on," Brooklyn said as she walked into the kitchen.

"Yo, I knew that nigga was pussy. What y'all take that nigga's lil ride for?"

"No, Daddy, stop playing."

"Yo, ain't Diamond pregnant with that nigga's baby?"

"Yeah, Daddy, but shit is crazy for her right now. She is here with me now. Daddy, that's not the half. She just found out that Shymeek gave her HIV. When are you coming to get me?" Brooklyn asked.

"I'll be to get you in about a half hour."

"Aight, Daddy. I'll tell you everything when you get here. And Daddy, I need you to do me a big favor."

"What's that, boo?"

"I need you to let Diamond and Angel stay at one of your apartments."

"Baby, you know I don't have any problems with that. Diamond and Angel are family. I'll talk to you when I get there. Aight. Peace!"

After Brooklyn got off the phone with Divine, she walked into her bedroom to check on Diamond and Diamond was gone. She went to check the bathroom and Diamond wasn't there either. Brooklyn went upstairs to see if Diamond went up there to talk with her grandmother. Her nanna was fast asleep. Brooklyn walked into her son's room and he was asleep in his bed with his lil cousin. Brooklyn checked everywhere and Diamond was nowhere to be found. A funny feeling came over Brooklyn, so she went back downstairs and went into her closet to check her shoebox where she kept her 380 handgun that Divine had given her after the shooting at his house in Queens. The gun was gone. Brooklyn ran to the phone and called Divine back.

• • •

When Diamond awoke in a cold sweat from another one of her nightmares of Rahmel's abuse, she got out of Brooklyn's bed, went into Brooklyn's closet and took down the shoebox in which Brooklyn stashed the gun that Divine had given her. Diamond had her mind made up. Shymeek was going to pay for what he did to her.

Diamond peeped out of Brooklyn's bedroom door and watched to see if the coast was clear. As soon as Brooklyn disappeared into the kitchen, Diamond made her move to the door. She had made her mind up and didn't want Brooklyn trying to stop her. This was something she felt she *had* to do. "This nigga fucked up my life," Diamond said to herself as she walked the dangerous streets of Brooklyn, from Bedstuy to Brownsville, with Brooklyn's robe and slippers on. She had the 380 in her shorts pocket. When Diamond entered Shymeek's block, two young guys who were on the corner hustling tried to holla at her as she walked by them. "Y'all don't want me. I have the monster!" Diamond replied and kept walking.

"Damn, ma! That's fucked up," one of the hustlers said as he continued to serve the fiend he had copping from them.

Diamond entered Shymeek's front yard and checked her pockets for the keys. She pulled the keys out of her back pocket and entered the house. As Diamond entered the house, she heard the water running in the bathroom. Diamond tiptoed towards the bathroom as Shymeek was standing at the sink brushing his teeth preparing to get in the shower.

"Shymeek!" she screamed.

Shymeek jumped. When he turned around, he noticed Diamond standing in the doorway of the bathroom. He realized she had a gun in her hand.

"Diamond, what are you doing?" he asked with toothpaste dripping from his mouth.

"Mutha fucka, it's time for your punk ass to answer for what you did to me." Diamond gripped the gun with both hands and swayed side to side readying herself for whatever was to come.

"Diamond, hold up. Don't do nothing crazy. Let's talk. We can work through this." Shymeek tried to plead with Diamond.

"Let's talk?! What happened to all that *bitch this* and *bitch that* shit you was talking about over the phone?" Diamond said as she aimed the gun at Shymeek and pulled the trigger.

POP!!!

Shymeek fell to the ground screaming. "Arrgh!" He thought he'd been shot.

"Diamond, please, wait a minute." He gasped, took a deep breath and swallowed hard. He then checked himself for any bullet holes.

Diamond walked over to Shymeek, stood over him and pointed the 380 at Shymeek's head.

"You committed a *homo*-cide. You murdered me. I'm dead. You gave me a death sentence, nigga," Diamond said as she kicked Shymeek in the face.

Diamond looked down at the punk who was supposed to

be her knight in shining armor. Calmly she spoke. "Shymeek, that was fucked up what you did to me, to our baby." She kept the gun pointed at him. "You killed us. We're fuckin' dead!" She was crying again. "But you know what?" Diamond wiped the tears from her face with her free hand and continued to speak. "It's all good. I'ma be aight. I'ma fight this shit. I've been through too much to let a faggot, pussy, gay ass, bitch nigga stop me from living. I'm too strong, Shymeek, and I can live with this, can you?" And with that, Diamond slapped Shymeek with the barrel of her 380, knocking him unconscious. She looked down at him, spat on his back, frowned, called him a *bitch ass nigga* and walked out of his house.

• • •

When Divine reached Brooklyn's house, Brooklyn was at the door waiting for him. Brooklyn had a worried look on her face. Brooklyn told Divine everything that Shymeek had done to Diamond. And then she told Divine about Diamond leaving and taking the gun out of the shoebox. Brooklyn jumped into Divine's car and they drove to Shymeek's house.

About two blocks from where Shymeek lived, Brooklyn and Divine spotted Diamond walking casually as if she didn't have a care in the world.

"Diamond," Brooklyn yelled to her friend as Divine was pulling over.

Diamond recognized Divine's car and her best friend's voice, and immediately ran over to where her friends were.

Brooklyn jumped out of the car and she and Diamond hugged one another and started crying. They buried their faces in each other's shoulders and acknowledged each other's feelings for the other through their tears.

Divine kept to the side and let the girls have their moment.

Chapter 19
Time's Up!

Rahmel had Mike and Red drive him around all night until they found Angel up in a crackhead's apartment getting high. Rahmel had bribed a fiend with fifty dollars and she took Rahmel right to Angel. Angel was in the crib smoking the last of the crack rock that she had from tricking with a local drug dealer. When Rahmel walked into the house, Angel never once looked up to even notice Rahmel enter the room.

"Yo, come on, Angel, it's time to go," Rahmel said as he snatched the stem she was smoking the rock in from her hand.

Angel frantically rushed Rahmel without realizing who he was. She tried to get back her stem so she could finish the last of her rock. Rahmel grabbed her and threw her to the floor. That's when Angel realized that it was Rahmel with whom she was tussling. The fiend in whose apartment they were fighting tried to protest, but Red pulled out his gun and smacked her across the face with it. "Shut up, bitch, and sit down," Red said as he watched his man pin Angel to the floor.

"Let me go, Rahmel. Fuck you. It's because of you that I'm like this. You destroyed my life."

"Angel, fuck that right now. That's not the issue. The issue is you being here killing yourself. You are still my wife and I can't stand to see you like this. Come on, let's go."

Angel tried her best to fight Rahmel off of her, but her frail frame didn't have the strength. This was due to the fact that she was exhausted from the strain and abuse she put on her body, not to mention her just awaking out of a coma. Angel collapsed and Rahmel snatched her up and took her home.

Once Rahmel got Angel to the house that was once *their* house, he prepared a hot bath for her so she could clean herself up. At first, Angel didn't like the fact that Rahmel had brought her back to the house from which she and Diamond had escaped over three years ago. Then guilt kicked in about her actually being there with Rahmel and she felt at ease. Of all the people she ever thought that would come to her rescue, Rahmel would have been the last person that would have come to her mind. Angel knew that she needed help. Crack had a tight hold on her. She didn't care about anything except smoking, and that scared her. While Angel took a hot bath, Rahmel was in the kitchen cooking up an ounce of raw cocaine into crack rock. If getting high was what Angel wanted to do, she would never have to trick to get what she wanted as long as he was in power to support her habit. Whatever she did to get her high, she wouldn't have to go outside of the house to do so. She could trick with him.

Rahmel told Mike and Red that they could leave. "Yo, I'll come and get y'all in the morning." Rahmel escorted them to the door. It was time for him to be alone with his Angel who he had been missing ever since the day that she and Diamond left him. There wasn't a night that had passed that he didn't think about Angel. Once she left him, Rahmel realized how much he really loved her. When she first had Rahmel arrested for domestic abuse, his first reaction was to kill her if he ever saw her again. But as the years passed and no Angel, his anger turned to guilt and loneliness. He had her back now even though she was strung out on the very drug that he made his living off of. He wasn't trying to lose her again. As soon as Rahmel finished cooking up the cocaine into rock, he went into the bathroom where Angel was laid back soaking herself in a bath of hot water.

• • •

After Brooklyn, Divine and Diamond left Shymeek's area, they drove to Divine's house in New Jersey. Brooklyn was exhausted. She had watched her best friend's life fall apart right in front of her eyes. As soon as the girls entered the house, they sat on Divine's plush couch and started crying once again. Brooklyn felt Diamond's pain and hurt. The fact that she couldn't do anything for her friend made her feel even worse. Divine went into the room to check on Heaven, who was comfortably tucked under her sheets fast asleep. Divine kissed her on the cheek and quietly tiptoed out of her room. Divine went back into the living room, lifted Brooklyn up and carried her into the bedroom. Diamond walked over to a pile of blankets, picked one up, wrapped it around herself, laid down on the comfortable sofa and fell asleep.

As Divine laid Brooklyn on the bed, he started undressing her. As he undressed her, he placed small teasing kisses, bites and nibbles on Brooklyn's breasts, ears, neck and stomach. Brooklyn moaned at Divine's touch. As Divine took Brooklyn's thong off, he focused all of his attention on Brooklyn's clitoris. When Divine started licking the inner walls of Brooklyn's womanhood, his cell phone started ringing.

"Oooohhh! Daddy answer your phone," Brooklyn moaned as Divine darted his tongue in and out of her sweetness. Brooklyn moaned as her toes curled and she squeezed and pulled at Divine's hair. "Ooowww, shit! Divine, please stop. You have to answer your phone. It might be important," Brooklyn said as she pushed Divine's head from between her legs.

Divine got up and answered the phone. He wiped his mouth and gave Brooklyn a smile.

"Yo, who's this?" he asked. His face became serious.

"Vine, it's Remo."

"Yo, Remo, what's poppin', dog?"

"Yo, God, as we was coming back from taking care of that bitch, the 5.0 tried to pull us over."

"Word! What happened?"

"You know what happened, we did what we had to do. That's why you're talking to me now. But Gangsta is dead and Byheem took one. The police got him."

"Y'all meet me at the house in Queens. Whop and I-Shine are there right now. Give me about forty-five minutes."

"Aight. Peace!" Remo said.

Divine hung up the phone and started fixing his clothes.

"Daddy, is everything alright?" Brooklyn asked.

"Yeah, boo, I have to make a move real quick. I'll be back."

"Daddy, let me go with you. I know you're up to something and I have bad vibes about tonight."

"Boo, don't worry about it. Everything is gonna be alright. I got good people around me."

"I know, Daddy, but they're not willing to put their lives on the line for you like I am. Let me go with you, Daddy, let me protect you."

"Nah, boo, I need you home with my daughter, to take care of her if anything happens to me. Diamond needs you to be here for her too. Just hold the fort down, boo."

"That's what I'm talking about, Daddy. What do you mean

if anything happens to you? Please, Daddy, don't go. If you do, let me go with you," Brooklyn begged.

"Nah, Queen, this is where I need you to be." Divine pulled out a certified envelope from his coat pocket and passed it to Brooklyn. "Brooklyn, do you know what this is? This is a will and instructions to my lawyers. And do you know who the benefactor is? You, and I hold you responsible for Heaven," Divine said as he turned to leave out the door.

"Divine, hold up. Since I can't talk you out of going or letting me go with you, here." Brooklyn handed Divine a piece of paper with an address on it. "Daddy, this is Rahmel's address."

"Word, Mommy. How you get this info?" Divine grabbed the piece of paper and looked at the information written on it.

"Daddy, he lives in the same house that he lived in since Diamond was a baby."

"Thanks, Ma, I love you. I'll see you in a few." Divine gave Brooklyn a kiss and headed out the door.

Brooklyn laid back on the bed and hoped that she didn't make the wrong decision as far as giving Divine Rahmel's address. Brooklyn hoped that she didn't jeopardize her friendship with Diamond by getting the information out of her about her father's whereabouts and giving it to Divine, knowing that Divine was going to kill him. *Fuck that nigga, he need to die for what he did to Angel and Diamond anyway*, Brooklyn reasoned with herself for her actions.

• • •

Rahmel walked into the bathroom while Angel was relaxing in the bath, contemplating her life.

"Angel, how are you feeling?" he asked in a cordial manner.

"I don't know, Rahmel, I don't know if it's the right thing or not for me to be here with you."

"Angel, you are still my wife. I want the best for you." Rahmel tried to convince her.

"Rahmel, you have destroyed my life. I never got over what you have done to me and how you just abandoned us." She rolled her eyes at him and lowered herself in the water until only her head was visible.

"Angel, I didn't abandon you. Y'all left me, remember? You had *me* locked up."

"That's because you abused me for fifteen years and then you started abusing your daughter. We had to leave you."

"Listen, let's not go through this right now. I brought you something to ease your pain. Let's just enjoy each other's company for old time sakes. And if by the morning you still feel the same way, then you would never have to worry about me again. But for now, let me show you a good time," Rahmel said as he pulled from behind him the ounce of cooked up rock on a plate.

Angel's eyes opened wide when she saw what Rahmel had in his hand. Rahmel passed Angel a stem and a lighter. As Angel took the glass dick into her mouth and inhaled, Rahmel played with her nipples, stuck his hand into her bath water and started finger popping her.

Rahmel got undressed as Angel put the stem up to his lips. He inhaled crack for the first time. Fuck it, he was with his Angel and they were going to enjoy the night together. As Rahmel inhaled the smoke of crack, he got a rush. His dick became hard as a brick so he slammed another rock into the pipe. Angel took his manhood into her mouth. Although Angel would never forgive Rahmel for the years of abuse he had put her through, right now he was *the man* standing in front of her with a plate full of rock. And she was willing to do whatever he wanted her to do. She wanted to smoke every crumb on the plate. And if Rahmel wanted her to be the Angel that he used to love, she would be just that.

• • •

On the sofa in Divine's living room, Diamond woke up to a sharp pain in her stomach as she felt hot fluid running down her leg. Diamond looked down and noticed that she was bleeding. Diamond started screaming for Brooklyn that she was losing her baby. Diamond knew that she was having a miscarriage and Brooklyn came running to her aid. When Brooklyn reached the living room, Diamond collapsed from the pain and exhaustion.

• • •

When Divine reached the house in Queens, Whop, I-Shine, Kali, Remo and Mo'Better were all sitting in the living room smoking blunts and talking about the night's events. When Divine entered the crib, he was bombarded with the smell of that sticky that he knew only Mo'Better smoked from the Juice Bar uptown.

"What's poppin'?" he asked the crowd.

"Yo, blood, shit went crazy," Kali said as he passed the blunt he was smoking to Divine.

"Yo, God, on our way back from smoking that traitor bitch China, the po po had the nerve to try and pull us over. And you know we couldn't have that, son. Not when we just finished smoking a mutha fucka and we had all the guns in the car with us. So we did what we had to do, we started dumping on them pigs. Ya heard? But the fucked up part is that they murdered Gangsta and Byheem got hit."

"Is Byheem dead?" Divine asked, concerned.

193

"We don't know. After we murdered one of the cops and we saw Gangsta's head split wide open, I saw Byheem go down, but I don't know if he got killed. Me and Remo jumped in the hooptie and got the fuck up out of there."

"If Byheem lived, we don't have to worry about him. He'll hold his head. He's broke from that type of cloth. He's true to the game," Divine said as he passed Whop the *L*.

"Yo, God, Whop and I-Shine told us how y'all handled that nigga Alfonso and got the work back."

"Yeah, God, that shit was a work of art," Divine said as he gave Remo a pound.

"Yo, Vine, this is for you, baby," Mo'Better said as he placed two suitcases on the table in front of him filled with money.

"That's what I'm talking about. Yeah. Ayo, Mo', I need you right now. You know this little war shit is slowing up my cash flow. But after tonight, all that shit should be dead. Ya heard?"

"What's up, Vine, what ya need me to do, baby? Talk to me." Mo'Better rubbed his hands together emphasizing his anxiety.

"Yo, son, I need you to take a hundred of these things off my hands for me. Do you think you can swing it?" Divine asked.

"No doubt! Just give me a lil more time and I'll have every dime of your money right."

"Aight, that's what I'm talking about fam. Yo, Remo, take Mo'Better to the warehouse and give him what he needs and drop this dough off at my house in New Jersey. If Brooklyn asks you where I'm at, tell her that you didn't see me. Tell her that this was something that you had for me. Me, Whop, I-Shine and Kali are going to see that nigga Rahmel tonight,"

Divine said to Remo as he gave him the two suitcases and the keys to his 600.

"Word, son, I wanna get that nigga too."

"Nah, Remo, I need you to handle that with Mo'Better. Me, Whop, I-Shine and Kali can handle this old ass nigga. Ya heard?"

Remo and Mo'Better left the crib and Divine and them planned their move. It was time.

• • •

When Remo and Mo'Better left the crib, Remo jumped in Divine's 6 and Mo'Better jumped in his ride. As Remo pulled off, Mo'Better looked back and gave a signal to a car that was parked a couple of cars behind his in the cut. As Mo'Better pulled off to follow Remo, the car in the cut pulled off as well.

Things were going better than Mo'Better had planned. The plan was to send Sanders and his lil *take money crew* into the house and lay everybody down and take whatever money and drugs that were in the house including the money that Mo'Better had just given him. Mo'Better knew that at any given time, Divine could have anywhere from a hundred thousand to five hundred thousand in his house.

Big Sanders had just come home from doing sixteen years in federal prison. Sanders and his crew's name rang bells in Harlem. So when he came home and found out that a nigga from Brooklyn was running shit in Harlem, Big Sanders made it his business to step to Mo'Better. Big Sanders told Mo'Better that if he put him onto his supplier, that his crew could eat in Harlem without any problems. Mo'Better knew of Sanders and his crew and knew that they didn't play. So Mo' agreed only if he could keep whatever drugs that were taken and Sanders would keep the money.

Divine was his man from back in the days, but fuck it, this was the game. There's no honor amongst thieves. So Divine was just a stepping stool in his climb to the top. Mo'Better didn't expect to hit the jackpot. He knew after this, he would have to murder Divine. To hit Divine's warehouse was huge, not to mention that he just got back over two hundred keys from that nigga Alfonso. If they played it right, they could force Remo to take them to Divine's house where he had the mother load stashed. Mo'Better smiled to himself as he followed Remo.

Chapter 20

Let's Get 'em!

Divine, Whop, I-Shine and Kali pulled behind a van that was parked a couple of houses down from Rahmel's house. They walked at a fast pace and entered Rahmel's yard. The front door to Rahmel's house took Whop less than a minute to crack open. "Yeah, let's get this nigga," Whop said in a whisper as they all rushed into the house with their guns out. All the lights in the house were out except the bathroom lights and they heard moaning coming from that direction.

"Yo," Divine said as he waved Whop and I-Shine to go check the back as he motioned for Kali to follow him toward the bathroom. As they opened the bathroom door, Angel was straddling Rahmel's cock as he sat on the toilet. Angel had her eyes closed as Rahmel fucked her in the ass from behind. As soon as Angel heard the bathroom door open up, she opened her eyes and noticed two armed men standing in the doorway pointing guns. Angel couldn't place where she knew one of the armed men's face from. Before it registered to her, Rahmel jumped up and opened his eyes. Kali reacted to Rahmel's movement and squeezed the trigger.

POP, POP, POP, POP, POP, POP!!!

"Nooooo!" Rahmel screamed as Angel's body was rattled with bullets. Rahmel suddenly lunged at Kali with surprising speed. Rahmel seemed to have had no fear of the fact that someone was standing in his bathroom door with guns pointed at him. The fact that they had just killed Angel had Rahmel react in a blind fury.

POP, POP, POP, POP, POP!!!

Kali continued to fire several more shots, hitting Rahmel in the body and chest. But Rahmel refused to go down. He rushed Kali, grabbed him in a bear hug and tussled him to the floor. Rahmel bit into Kali's jugular vein. Kali screamed out in pain and agony as Rahmel locked on his neck like a pit bull and started ripping and tearing into his flesh.

BUNG, BUNG, BUNG!!!

Divine stood over them as he fired three shots to the back of Rahmel's head. Rahmel's body slumped lifeless on top of Kali as I-Shine and Whop ran into the bathroom. They helped Divine yank Rahmel's dead weight off of Kali. Kali was holding his neck as his body shook and convulsed. His blood shot out from between his fingers. The blood poured steadily from his neck. It was too late for Kali. They watched him take his final breath.

"Oh, shit! Nooo!" Everybody quickly turned around and looked at Divine to see what the problem was. Divine stood over Angel's body checking her for a pulse.

"Yo, God, what the fuck are you doing? We got to get the fuck out of here," Whop said as he pulled on Divine's shirt.

Divine had recognized Angel as she lay in her own pool of blood. "Yo, this is Diamond's mother, Angel. Fuck! What the fuck was she doing here?" Divine was stricken with grief, as he was bent over checking her for any vital signs. She was dead.

Whop grabbed Divine. "Yo, let's get out of here. It's too

late for her." Divine snapped out of it and he, I-Shine and Whop ran out of the bathroom.

• • •

Mike and Red sat in front of their building shooting dope. They had left their keys on Rahmel's living room table. They couldn't get into their apartment so they decided to get high in the car instead of rushing back to Rahmel's crib. They wanted to give him a little time to be with Angel. However, when they were out of dope and couldn't get into their apartment to get the rest of their shit, they had to go back to Rahmel's house to get their keys. As they pulled up in front of Rahmel's crib, Red jumped out to go get their keys when they heard gunshots. Mike got out the car and they both pulled out their gats as they noticed Rahmel's door wide open. When they entered the house, Divine, I-Shine and Whop came running out the bathroom.

BLAT, BLAT, BLAT...POP, POP, POP, POP, POP...BLAT, BLAT, BLAT!!!!

Divine and I-Shine, who were first to exit the bathroom, both hit the floor. Whop jumped behind the door and returned fire hitting Red in the head. Mike continued to fire as he backed out of the house. Mike hated leaving his brother, but he was already dead and Rahmel wasn't worth both of them dying. Mike jumped into his car and pulled off.

"Yo, come on y'all, we got to get out of here before the police come," Whop said as he ran over to Divine who was laying on the floor in a pool of his blood. "Noooo! Aw, no, Divine," Whop said as he snatched up his closest friend. Blood poured from two holes in Divine's chest close to his heart. Divine died in Whop's arms. Whop looked over and noticed I-Shine was dead as well. Whop shed tears as he closed Divine's

eyes. "Rest in peace, God. I got your family for you, soldier."
Whop laid his man down and ran out the crib.

• • •

Remo pulled up in front of the warehouse as Mo'Better
pulled in behind him. As Remo opened the door of the warehouse, a black Beamer pulled up and four men jumped out
pointing guns at Remo. When Remo reached for his shit,
Mo'Better hit Remo in the back of the head with the butt of his
gun. Remo dropped and Mo'Better and Sanders carried him
inside the building. Mo'Better and Sanders tied Remo up to a
chair that was sitting in the office as Sanders' crew searched the
warehouse.

"Yo, we found it," one of Sanders' boys hollered as they
entered a van that was parked toward the back of the warehouse. "Damn! This nigga was holding like Peru."

Mo'Better and Sanders walked over to the van. "Yo, how
the fuck we gonna get all this shit out of here?" Sanders asked
as he looked in the van.

"We gonna use the van," Mo'Better said as he looked for
a screwdriver in the glove compartment of the van.

"Yo, where is all the money you was telling us about,
nigga?" Sanders asked as he looked Mo'Better in the eyes with
distrust.

"Calm down, son. We gonna have this nigga show us
where that nigga Divine lives. He keeps millions in his house,"
Mo'Better said as he walked over to where they had Remo tied
up and slapped him in the face a couple of times to wake him
up.

As Remo came to, he could feel the hot blood running
down his neck from his head wound. Remo tried to focus but
felt woozy from the blow to his head. "Yo, Mo', what the fuck

is going on?" He didn't want to believe what was happening to him.

"Nigga, you know what this is. We already have the drugs, but we want to know where Divine lives in New Jersey."

Remo looked around the warehouse and noticed the four dudes that jumped out the BMW. "Yo, Mo', you know Divine is gonna kill you and your whole family for this, don't you?"

CRACK!!

Remo's head jerked back as Sanders smacked him in the face with his gun. "Bitch, lil nigga. Shut the fuck up! Just answer the fucking question."

"Mutha fucka, you might as well kill me because I'm not telling y'all bitch asses shit about my man. I'm true to the end," Remo said as he spit his blood into Sanders' face.

BUNG...BUNG, BUNG, BUNG!!!

"Yo, why you kill him? How are we gonna get the money?"

"Fuck the money. We got the drugs," Sanders said as he turned to Mo'Better pointing his gun.

BUNG! BUNG! BUNG!

"Die like the snake in the grass you are," Sanders said as he spit on Mo'Better. He told two of his boys to jump in the van and hotwire it as he and his other man ran outside and jumped in the BMW. He waited for them to come out of the warehouse with the van and then they all pulled off.

Chapter 21

A Priceless Jewel

One year later ...

Brooklyn pulled her candy apple red Bentley GT to the corner of 141st Street and Amsterdam in Manhattan where Diamond was handing out flyers for the evening's events. She parked and got out.

"Excuse me." Diamond stopped a young college student who was on here way to class. City College was one block over. "Are you a student at City College?" Diamond asked her.

The young lady nodded and focused her eyes on the flyer that Diamond had in her hand. Diamond handed it to her. "It's AIDS awareness month and we're having a seminar this evening with some special guests."

The girl accepted the flyer from Diamond and asked her, "Where is this lecture thing gonna take place and what time will it be starting?" She was looking at the flyer, occasionally glancing back at Diamond.

Diamond looked at her friend Brooklyn and said, "B.K., hold on a second, I'm trying to convince this young lady here to join us tonight." Diamond pointed at the girl but was looking over at Brooklyn. "Anyway, Ma," Diamond reverted her attention back to the young lady standing in front of her. "We'll be at *THE BROOKLYN HOUSE* tonight and the event starts at 7 p.m.

"What side is *THE BROOKLYN HOUSE* on, the east side or the west?" the girl asked.

"The east side, baby!" Brooklyn yelled from the sideline smiling.

THE BROOKLYN HOUSE was an auditorium that was built in the college, paid for by Brooklyn herself from the money Divine had left her. The auditorium was named after her because of the effort she put into making it become one of the most occupied sectors of the school. It was reserved for seminars, lectures, speeches and meetings that dealt with increasing awareness of HIV and AIDS in all communities.

The girl accepted a flyer, smiled and said, "I'll be there," before catching her next class.

Diamond tucked the remaining flyers in her purse, grabbed Brooklyn's hand and led her toward the school. "Yeah, she'll be there," Diamond said to Brooklyn, referring to the student. "The singer *MELSOULTREE* will be in the house too. She's supposed to perform something off of her new CD and then talk about how much she's helped in raising the awareness of HIV and AIDS." Diamond smiled at her friend.

Brooklyn stopped in the middle of the block, looked at Diamond who had a look on her face like *"What?"* and said, "Diamond, you have been a model of strength. A picture of courage and a symbol of hope. You truly are *A DIAMOND IN THE ROUGH* and the world could be a lot better if there were more Diamonds like yourself around." With that, the ladies took hold of each other's hands and strolled toward the campus.

THE END...

Real Talk

According to the CDC: The Center For Disease Control & Prevention

The leading cause of HIV infection among African-American men is sexual contact with another man.

The leading cause of HIV infection among African-American women is heterosexual contact.

In 2001, HIV infection was the leading cause of Death for African-American women aged 25-34 years, as well as hispanic women aged 35-44 years.

Through 2003, 170,679 women were given a diagnosis of AIDS.

An estimated 81,864 women with AIDS died.

African-American and Hispanic women together represent about 25% of all U.S. women, yet they account for 83% of AIDS diagnoses in 2003.

Amiaya Entertainment encourages all of our readers to go and get tested. Protect yourself, and your partner.

For more information call 1-866-rap-it-up

Fan Mail Page

If you have any further questions, comments or concerns,
kindly address your inquires in care of:

James "I-God" Morris
At

AMIAYA ENTERTAINMENT
P.O.BOX 1275
NEW YORK, NY 10159
tanianunez79@hotmail.com

or

Igodmorris@hotmail.com

Coming Soon

From
Amiaya Entertainment LLC

"I Ain't Mad At Ya"
by
Travis "Unique" Stevens

&

"Against The Grain"
by
G. B. Johnson

&

" Sister"
by
T. Benson Glover

www.amiayaentertainment.com

Flower's Bed

The Most Controversial Book Of This Era

Written By

Antoine "Inch" Thomas

Suspenseful...Fastpaced...Richly Textured

PUBLISHED BY AMIAYA ENTERTAINMENT

From the Underground Bestseller "Flower's Bed"
Author Antoine "Inch" Thomas delivers you

NO REGRETS

It's Time To Get It Popping

"Gritty....Realistic Conflicts....Intensely Eerie"
Published by Amiaya Entertainment

TRAVIS "UNIQUE" STEVENS
NY
AVAILABLE NOW FROM
AMIAYA ENTERTAINMENT
ISBN# 0-9745075-5-5
I AIN'T
MAD
AT
ya
PUBLISHED BY AMIAYA ENTERTAINMENT, LLC.

ALL OR NOTHING

MICHAEL WHITBY

PUBLISHED BY AMIAYA ENTERTAINMENT, LLC.

A STORY THAT WILL HAVE YOU ON YOUR TOES FROM BEGINING TO END...
AGAINST THE GRAIN
AVAILABLE NOW FROM
AMIAYA ENTERTAINMENT
ISBN# 0-9745075-6-3
G.B. JOHNSON
PUBLISHED BY AMIAYA ENTERTAINMENT, LLC.

So Many Tears

Teresa Aviles

PUBLISHED BY AMIAYA ENTERTAINMENT, LLC.

HOE-ZETTA
VINCENT WARREN BRINGS YOU ANOTHER "HOT" NOVEL FROM AMIAYA ENTERTAINMENT
AVAILABLE NOW FROM
AMIAYA ENTERTAINMENT
ISBN# 0-9745075-8-X
VINCENT "V.I." WARREN
PUBLISHED BY AMIAYA ENTERTAINMENT, LLC.